Club Force

Pamela Duncan

Club Force

By Pamela Duncan

cover design by Andrew Skinner

Published by Author Way Limited

Copyright © 2015 Pamela Duncan
All rights reserved.

ISBN-10:   1512355798
ISBN-13-   978-1512355796

Dedication

Club Force is dedicated to the members of Caldwell Golf Club, Uplawmoor, East Renfrewshire with whom I've spent many happy hours battling the Fairways and Greens. Caldwell is a delightful, challenging, country course and its membership is a friendly band of law-abiding citizens, unlike some of those at the fictional Fisborough Course.

Caldwell members might recognise certain aspects of the layout of Fisborough, but there are differences and all the characters portrayed in Club Force are a figment of my imagination, although the Christian names of Sheenagh, Agnes and Josie are included by request.

Acknowledgements

Thanks go to Sheila and Stewart for proof reading, to Andrew for producing the cover and to a certain ex police officer, turned taxi driver, for advice on police procedures.

A big thank you goes to my ever patient publishers for their continued support.

This book has been brought to you by -

Author **way**

Discover other Author Way Limited titles at –

www.authorway.net

Or to contact the author email to: info@authorway.net

Club Force is a work of fiction written by Pamela Duncan. No characters or criminal events in the book are real and any similarity to people and events, living or dead is purely coincidental.

Table of Contents

Club Force

Also by Pamela Duncan:

> On the Swing of One Star

> The Secret of the Long Room

About the author

About Author Way Limited

CHAPTER 1

August bathed the Fisborough Golf Club in mid-morning sunshine. It was too good a day to waste. Nick Baker consulted his watch as he waited impatiently beside the first tee.

"Nearly ten past ten. Where the devil has Carlton got to?" he asked Grant Mason, who along with Carlton Greenhalgh made up a three in the regular Sunday round.

Grant shook his head, and spoke to two middle-aged lady members pulling their clubs on trolleys.

"You'd better go ahead of us, girls," he said. "We're still waiting for Carlton."

"Late is he?" the taller of the ladies commented, smugly. "I understood your past captain was a stickler for time keeping. I saw his wife's car a while back, but I expect they came separately." She turned to her partner, "Come along, it's your honour." She took out her Big Bertha driver and had a few practice swings as her golfing buddy stepped on to the tee.

Nick's eyes narrowed at their indifferent shots. "Could be a long round behind those two. Hope they let us through. I could kill Carlton."

"That's a bit strong." Grant wandered to the end of the path and called back, "No sign of him coming."

Nick paced up and down for a further three minutes before saying, "I vote we start without him. We can leave a message with Dougie." Without waiting for a response, Nick went into the professional's shop. Seconds later he came out smiling. "Dougie's away to the toilet or somewhere. I've told his young assistant to let Carlton know. I expect he'll catch up on us at the third. By the way, the lad swears he saw Carlton around earlier. Guess he's had to go back home for something."

Nick stood on the first tee. The ladies were still battling their way to the green. He watched them irritably before deciding it was safe to play. Tall, slim and athletic for his forty-odd years, he sent a beautiful drive up the middle. Grant, shorter, stockier and into his early fifties, matched the shot. The pair set off up the fairway, casting shadows on the well cropped grass. Not a breath of wind disturbed the trees. It was a perfect golfing day.

As Nick and Grant disappeared in the distance, a lone figure raced down the 18th fairway towards the club house. White faced and panting despite his wiry build, Bradley Brown grabbed Dougie Watson, the professional, as he returned to the shop.

He had just enough breath left in his lungs to blurt out, "There's a guy lying out there with his head covered in blood."

"What? Was he hit by a ball?"

"I doubt it. Too much blood. It's bad I tell you."

"Who is it? Do you know?"

"He's lying face down. Not immediately recognisable. I didn't stop for a close look. We're wasting time. He needs an ambulance. Though I doubt it'll do him much good."

"You mean he's had it?"

"I wasn't feeling for a pulse through all that gore, but I

reckon he's a goner. Get on the blower. Someone has to cover him up before any of the ladies find him."

"Where exactly is he?"

"The long rough on the left hand side of the seventeenth. That is right hand going up from here. A bit above the practice area. My clubs are still there. I dropped them and ran. You can't see him from the fairway. I'd never have found him if I hadn't duffed my drive miles left. Come on, man, we can't just leave him out there."

Dougie, a laid back lad, early twenties, blonde, tall, broad shouldered and powerful, had gained a reputation for keeping his cool in the few months he'd been club pro'. He thought before acting. Having ordered his assistant to keep the shop going, he led Brad round to the Secretary's office to repeat the story. A suitably astounded James Winter, aware of Brad's past pranks as club wag, was cautious.

"No chance you could be mistaken Bradley? This isn't one of your little jokes, I hope?"

"Do you think I'm a nutter?" Brad replied. "For heaven's sake look at me? I don't shake like this for nothing. Here, give me the phone and I'll get help myself."

James Winter adjusted his spectacles and adopted an air of authority. "No need for that, Bradley. Sorry. I'll attend to things." He lifted the telephone and dialled for an ambulance.

"Get on to the police, too. That fellow didn't inflict that much damage on himself."

"Yes, of course."

"Now what?" Dougie asked once the necessary calls had been placed.

"We'd better go and see for ourselves. Perhaps you should stay here Bradley. Dougie and I will go. Get yourself a strong drink. You look pretty grim. But don't say anything. Not yet. Okay?"

"I'd rather go with you. I'm alright. And I've to pick up my clubs."

"We could do that," James offered.

Bradley Brown, however, was already heading through the trees alongside the eighteenth hole towards the spot where the unidentified body lay half buried in the deep rough.

James Winter informed the club steward that there had been an accident and an ambulance and the police would arrive shortly.

"Keep quiet about this until we know more. I shouldn't be away very long," the secretary told him.

James Winter was aware his grey business suit was out of place on the course as he strode beside Dougie. He felt uncomfortable on that score alone. Added to their mission, he was decidedly on edge and was relieved there were no golfers on the eighteenth to

pass comment. He'd seen dead men when he was in the services but this was different. He glanced at Dougie and marvelled at his composure. Bradley had reached his clubs by the time they caught up with him.

"He's over there near the chestnut tree," he said, tossing a golf ball from one hand to the other. "I found my other ball on the way up it wasn't as far in as I thought, unless it took a kindly bounce. If you don't mind I'll stay here."

"Good idea. Keep anyone who tries to see what we're up to at bay, there's a good fellow. Pretend you're still hunting for your ball or something."

"Not many of the early birds have reached this far. It's only ten-forty-five."

James and Dougie moved forward tentatively for some thirty metres to where Bradley indicated. It was a well sheltered spot with a low wall of tall grass and overgrown shrubs concealing it from the fairway. Twigs snapped under their feet and in the silence sounded like gun shots. A startled crow squawked and fluttered into flight. They came on the body suddenly. Face down, as Bradley had said, the head covered with a thick bloody ooze. The man's white visor, stained bright red, lay half on, half off, his head. He was wearing a non-distinctive navy blue polo shirt and fawn slacks.

"Could be anyone," James said.

Dougie lent forward over the body. "You're wrong there, Mr Winter. It's Carlton Greenhalgh. I sold him those shoes a few days ago. See the green circle round the studs? They're a brand new design. I only had the one pair as an advance and let Carlton have them. You can't get them anywhere else yet, I'm positive. The rep said so. And see, he's Carlton's build."

James Winter paled as recognition dawned on him. "I think you're right, Dougie."

Dougie lifted the man's wrist. "No sign of a pulse. Gone, I'm afraid." He turned the man's head slightly. "I was right. It is Carlton."

Dougie wiped his blood-stained fingers on the grass to clean them. The sound of sirens getting closer and closer signalled the simultaneous arrival of the police and an ambulance. Any chance of keeping the incident quiet was shattered.

"I must get down there," James Winter said. "Could you face staying with the.... with Carlton? I'll persuade Bradley to carry on keeping the coast clear."

The club secretary spoke to Bradley before walking, somewhat unsteadily, back to the club house. The flashing lights and sirens had brought everyone out onto the forecourt. James Winter braced himself to speak to the police sergeant and his constable.

"Thank you for coming so promptly. There's been a terrible accident..... er... tragedy. Just step into my office and I'll explain."

Once in his sanctum, he related the morning's events as he knew them. "I've left Dougie Watson, the professional, up there with the body and one of our members is keeping other golfers at bay. Making sure nothing is disturbed."

"Thank you, Mr Winter. We'll take over now." The trio stepped outside. "Can you arrange for everyone to go into the building and I'd be pleased if you'd draw up a list of names and addresses of all those on the premises. Ask them to hang around. We'll need to take statements and say as little as possible. Tell them I'll speak to them when I come back. The course has to be closed from now on and catch players as they finish their rounds. Try not to let anyone leave the premises. Well, I think that's all for the moment. Now, point me in the right direction, please."

James Winter indicated the way. "You'll see our two men up there."

The police officers set off followed by two ambulance men carrying a stretcher and the club secretary turned to the group that had gathered.

"The Sergeant wants you all to go inside and wait. I suggest we use the dining lounge," James ushered them through the door. "I'm sorry about this," he advised the steward. "We'll need to arrange for the course to close for play. Can't do anything about those already out, I'm afraid. We'll bring them in here as they finish their rounds."

"What's happened? It looks pretty serious?" The present club captain, Clive Meechan, a six-footer with silver hair and a full moustache, wanted to know.

"Sorry, I'm not at liberty to say."

"Come on, James, you can tell me...."

James Winter shook his head. He turned to the members sitting at the small tables dotted around the pleasant lounge, which doubled as a bar-dining room. "I'll circulate a sheet of paper. The Sergeant requires you all to put down your names and addresses. Might be a good idea if you state when you arrived at the club. You'll learn what's happened soon enough, when the police return. If you want to play cards, there are several packs in the locker room cupboard." He addressed the steward, "Perhaps you could bring them through?

***

Sergeant Harry Barnes and Police Constable Gregg Thomas chatted as they made their way to the seventeenth rough. "Beautiful out here, isn't it. Pity crime has to spoil it. Do you play, Gregg?"

"Used to play a lot when I was a kid. Now only occasionally. Not here, mind. At Meadowsburn. It's run by the council."

"I haven't had my clubs out for over a year. Walking up here puts me in the notion. They passed a group of players and ignored their curious glances. "That could be our man over there, far right."

The pair made towards a figure scouring the grass as if looking for balls. Bradley Brown shook hands with the officers. "The body's a bit further in. Dougie's with him. He says it's Carlton Greenhalgh."

"Thank you, and you are?"

"Bradley Brown. I found him."

"Right. We'll need to talk with you later. You can go back to the clubhouse, now, and I know it won't be easy, but please say nothing about this meantime."

"No Sergeant. I won't say a word."

Bradley moved down the hill a short distance and hovered around to wait for Dougie.

The police officers reached the place where the club professional sat some metres from where Carlton Greenhalgh's body lay. He stood up as they approached.

"Dougie Watson, I believe?" Sergeant Barnes introduced himself. "Thanks for everything. You may go now, but stay either in your shop or in the lounge with the others." He repeated his request for no mention of what had occurred. "The less people know at this stage the better. I'll trust your discretion."

Dougie joined Bradley and together they walked over the warm grass.

"Bit of a rum business, isn't it?" Brad commented.

"You can say that again." The young professional wiped sweat from his forehead. "It was hot as hell sitting up there with a corpse at my feet. Real weird."

Brad agreed, "I threw up a couple of times. It fairly turned my stomach."

They brushed aside queries from a group of players coming off the last and Bradley waited as Dougie spoke to his assistant, Graham Livesay.

"I'm shutting shop. You'd better come with me."

Most eyes lifted as they entered the club's dining lounge.

Clive Meechan sidled up to them. "Any news?" he asked, hopefully.

Dougie shook his head and the golfer went back to the game of Bridge he'd set up. James Winter had elected to sit at a table beside a corner window, a little apart from the remainder of the room. Dougie and Brad joined him whilst Graham went across to a junior member playing alone on the pool table.

"I'll fetch you a brandy, Bradley. You look in need of it," James said. He turned to the professional. "Dougie?"

"You sit and I'll get them. What are you drinking?"

James ordered a whisky and water. All three were aware they were the fodder for the whisperings at the other tables. Brad's eyebrows rose when Dougie returned with his brandy, the whisky for James and a coke for himself.

"I'm not into the heavy stuff," the professional volunteered.

"Very commendable but you could have been pardoned for making an exception, today," James Winter observed. "How did you get on with the police? Watch it, Brad, this table's a bit wobbly," he added as Brad nearly skittered his drink.

It was Dougie who answered. "Hardly spoke to them. We were summarily dismissed."

"What do you make of it all?"

Dougie shrugged, "Has to be murder. It'll cause quite a stir."

Brad gulped at his brandy. "Do you think the press will pester us?"

"It will probably make tomorrow's nationals. Might not be bad for business. We're bound to have loads of people gawking around. Perhaps I should put up an extra sign. They might come into the shop."

James Winter looked disgusted. "I don't consider this is a time to think of profit young man."

"I'm not serious. Just trying to lift the doom and gloom. Look at Bradley? He still hasn't stopped shaking. Weeping isn't going to bring Carlton back. He was a bit of a bastard, anyway."

"He was a past captain. A respected member of this club for many years. Which reminds me, I'll have to lower the flag." James got up and moved swiftly away.

"You've trodden on his corns. He was pretty thick with Carlton at one time. Mind you, rumour has it they didn't see eye to eye when Carlton was captain. James likes to rule the roost and Carlton's a strong man...or was," Bradley corrected himself. "Takes a bit of getting used to, doesn't it?" Dougie had picked up a golf magazine from the window ledge and treated Brad's last remark as rhetorical.

There was a general buzz about the lounge and some members were becoming restless. Not surprisingly, Brad thought. They'd been robbed of their Sunday morning round and been cooped up for ages. He could think of worse places to be incarcerated than the lounge with its plush blue carpet and full length picture windows. And there was the bar. The ever flowing bar. He made his way over to it and ordered a second double brandy.

"You should eat something," the steward advised. "Especially if you plan to drive home later."

Brad considered his still heaving stomach and declined. He was aware of the talk at some of the tables he passed. All surmise and yet a lot of it was near the truth. He heard the words 'body' and 'accident', 'killed by a ball, probably'. 'Could have happened to any one of us'. 'Do you know who it is?' Naturally, the presence of the police and the ambulance had set imaginations rolling. Brad returned to his corner table and tried to control his hands from shaking. He'd need to steady up for the interviews when the sergeant and his constable came back. He looked out of the window and saw several more officers making their way up to the seventeenth. No doubt the reinforcements were going to comb the area like he'd seen on the television. He hoped none of them would tread on his vomit.

CHAPTER 2

Sergeant Barnes greeted Detective Chief Inspector Raymond Yates as he arrived at the incident site. "Barnes, Sir, pleased to meet you. We've a nice kettle of fish here for a Sunday morning. We've confirmed the man's dead, of course. I sent the ambulance men back to their van, meantime. We'll bleep them when you're through. I've a lad scouting for a weapon or anything relevant, for that matter."

DCI Yates ordered the officers who'd arrived with him to join in the area search. He leaned over the body of Carlton Greenhalgh.

"Looks like at least three blows. He must have had his back turned to the assailant. Doubt if he knew what was coming his way."

"Bit of a messy job, this," the sergeant said. "They're sending an incident van from Laureston. Thought we'd set it up there." He indicated an area some twenty metres away. "That ground's been combed thoroughly already."

Yates ran his hands through his thick dark hair. "Wonder how long he's been here?"

"No idea, Sir. But he couldn't have lain overnight there were a couple of showers early this morning. I'd say an hour or two at the most."

"Do you know the fellow?"

"No. I've been told he's Carlton Greenhalgh, a member

here."

"Any details of family?"

"Not yet, Sir. I came straight up here."

"Looks as if he was hit with something pretty solid. A metal bar, possibly a golf club?"

"Are you ruling out an accident then?"

"He could hardly be hit accidentally several times."

"No, of course not," Sergeant Barnes blushed. "I've never dealt with a murder before, Sir, in the twenty-two years I've been here. There's the van coming now."

The white mobile van eased its way up the hill and Detective Chief Inspector Yates guided it into the position indicated by Barnes.

"Could you bring the men in for a briefing?"

"Of course, Sir."

Sergeant Barnes spread the word and the police officers quickly assembled outside the incident van. The doctor had arrived and stated the obvious and a police photographer was taking shots of the body and its surroundings from all angles.

"I want this whole area tooth-combed. Keep your eyes open for a metal club or bar. Could be a golf club. Anything relevant is to be brought here immediately. There are a number of footprints near the body. Some of them will be easily eliminated. I'll arrange for casts to be taken. Until then don't approach that section. Right, Sergeant Barnes, will you nominate an officer to man the van and list what turns up?"

"I'd suggest Gregg Thomas."

"That's settled then. You'll find everything you need inside, officer. Even the Sunday papers. I'll keep in touch."

"Yes, Sir. Thank you, Sir."

"Get on with it then, men." As the police officers resumed their search of the rough, the DCI turned to

Sergeant Barnes, "Any problem with nosey members?"

"Not yet, Sir. We've attracted a few curious glances, but no-one's come right over. I've cordoned off a fair section and play's suspended for the day. A number of games were already out. We haven't called them in".

"Do you play yourself?"

"Golf, you mean, Sir? Well, I do when I can find the time, which isn't enough these days."

"Might fit in a round during the investigation, then." He looked towards the seventeenth fairway. "It's an absorbing game. Don't think one of that foursome has even noticed us. I've seen enough." He turned towards the photographer. "Have you finished?"

"Just about"

"Tell the ambulance crew to take him away, then."

Sergeant Barnes put in the call and the attendants moved swiftly into action.

"Ready? Right we'll get down to the clubhouse and start inquiries. I understand from that secretary fellow everyone's gathered in the dining lounge." DCI Yates said.

"That's right, Sir. I told them to make sure no-one left except in an emergency and certainly not without giving their details."

"Good man. We'll grab some lunch first."

Flanked by the police officers and carried on the stretcher by the ambulance crew, Carlton Greenhalgh made his last trip down the side of the fairway and past the eighteenth green. A green on which he had sometimes triumphed and had still been able to return an acceptable card. The ambulance slipped silently out of the car park. The lack of sirens indicated more clearly than words that its passenger was no longer an emergency case.

***

Detective Chief Inspector Yates and his team had been granted the use of the family room as an interview area. It was adjacent to the main lounge and separated by a glass partition. They sat down at a table with their backs to the curious assembly in the dining lounge.

Over a light lunch, the DCI asked for a full report from Sergeant Barnes.

"You appear to have handled things well. Would you like to work together with me on this one? Your local knowledge could prove useful."

"I'd like to stay with it, Sir, if that can be arranged. I've always fancied being involved in a case like this."

"Good, though Heaven knows why. Firstly, what do I call you other than Sergeant?"

"My name's Harry, Sir."

"Right then, Harry. You can drop the formalities when it's just you and me. Call me Raymond."

"Yes, Sir."

DCI Yates had been handed the list of names gathered by the secretary, James Winter, and was pleased to note it included details such as:- arrived at the clubhouse about 8.45am or didn't get here till after 10am. He studied it.

"Seems there are seventeen people in the lounge and possibly double that on the course. Can't dismiss any of them, of course, but it's quite possible the perpetrator made a quick exit. Winter, tells me there are around six hundred members, and there's the staff. Think of it, Harry. Six hundred suspects before we even look into his personal life. Obvious trouble with this case is too many people. We need to start eliminating. Once we've taken statements from the main characters, you can move swiftly through the unlikeliest. Rule out any with an alibi that's positively sound and notify me of the doubtfuls. Painstaking work, but it has to be done."

"I'll do my best." He declined to add Raymond. Familiarity didn't come easily.

"We'd better go through and have a word with them. I gather his family have been contacted?" the DCI said.

"I sent a couple of WPC's to inform his wife and stay with her until we can get to see her ourselves. The son's already here. He was playing, I understand. "

The hub-bub in the dining lounge died suddenly as the police officers entered.

DCI Raymond Yates' clear voice rang with authority.

"Your attention please. I'm Detective Chief Inspector Yates. No doubt you've been questioning the events of this morning and it seems the right time to put you in the picture. It isn't a pretty one. A club member, Carlton Greenhalgh ...." Yates paused as a gasp ran through the group, then repeated, "Carlton Greenhalgh was found dead on the golf course this morning. We have still to have a positive identification but there is no reason to doubt it is Mr Greenhalgh. I'm sorry to say foul play is suspected. We have a job to do here. Not a very pleasant one, I'm afraid. Each of you will be required to make a statement, either to me or Sergeant Barnes, before you leave. In the circumstances, I'm sure you will all co-operate."

He smiled weakly as he and Sergeant Barnes went back into the family room.

"That's one of the worst bits over. I hate breaking the news. We'll set up a couple of tables to form a desk. Close the curtains, Harry, never know, there might be a lip reader among that lot," he said flippantly. Flippancy, he found was a way of relaxing. Each case had its tensions and this one promised to be as stressful as most.

Barnes drew the heavy blue curtains across the partition,

affording complete privacy. He posted a constable at the door.

Detective Chief Inspector Yates shuffled his feet, loosened his tie slightly and beckoned Sergeant Barnes to sit beside him.

"Right, that's us ready. We'll see the chap that found him first."

"Bradley Brown. He's a bit of a ferret, small and wiry." Barnes turned to the constable on the door. "Show him in, please."

Bradley finished his third drink and, with a pat of encouragement from Dougie, went into the family room to face the inquisition. Colour had returned to his cheeks and they now appeared flushed. The alcohol may have helped to steady his nerves but its affect was evident as he took a seat opposite the police officers.

"We've a number of questions we have to ask you, Mr Brown. Your answers will be recorded and you'll be required to sign a statement later. You understand? It's quite informal at this stage. Nothing to be nervous about."

Bradley nodded and the police officer went through the formalities of name, address, age etc., checking it with the sheet he had in front of him.

"I see you arrived at the course at a quarter to eight. Had you a game lined up?"

"No. I wanted to practice. I wasn't intending to play a whole round. Just a few holes but the weather was so good I stayed out."

"What time did you start?"

"Must have been about five past eight. I hadn't booked a time. The tee was quiet."

"And were you practising with anyone else?"

"No."

"Were you aware of any other players on the course?"

"I was concentrating on my own game but I did notice two guys some way ahead. I lost them around the thirteenth or fourteenth. Maybe they went off. A lot of members do at that point if they're pressed for time."

"So when would you estimate you reached the seventeenth?"

"It was the back of ten. I'd skipped some holes, you see. My tee shot was straight but dead short. So I took another and it was well enough struck but a mile off line to the left."

"And then?"

"I walked up the fairway, played the first ball and went to look for the second."

"Did you find it?"

"Not at that time. I judged it had gone into the deep rough and went to search for it. When I didn't find it immediately I went further in and saw the body."

"Must have given you quite a scare?"

"You bet it did."

"Did you recognise the man?"

"No. He was facing the ground and his head was smothered in blood."

"So when did you learn the identity of the victim?"

"A while later when the club pro' told me."

"Now, back to when you first found the body. Did you see anyone or anything? Anyone running or walking away, for instance? Perhaps someone lower down the hill?"

"I wasn't looking. I certainly wasn't aware of anyone. I raced to the shop for help."

"And you didn't see a weapon of any kind? A piece of heavy metal or a golf club, even?"

"If I had it would still have been there."

"Quite. You came running down the eighteenth and into

the shop. Why didn't you run through the trees? It's quicker, I believe."

"I lifted my first ball and just came down the middle. And I didn't go into the shop. Dougie, he's the professional, was outside. As if he was going back to it from the club house or somewhere."

"Dougie is outside his shop and you tell him about the body. How did he react?"

"He was calm. A bit too calm for my liking. Slow to do anything. But that's his way. Laid back they call it."

"And then?"

"We spoke to Mr Winter, the secretary, and he sent for an ambulance and yourselves."

Yates stopped his interrogation for a full minute as he studied his notes. When he resumed questioning the line of inquiry took Bradley Brown by surprise.

"Did you like Carlton Greenhalgh, Mr Brown?"

The flush on Brad's cheeks deepened. "I didn't have a lot to do with him."

"I asked if you liked him?" the detective persisted.

"Not particularly."

"Did you have any reason to dislike him?"

Brad shook his head, "Not really."

"Or know of anyone who might have wanted him dead?"

"No." The reply was almost snapped back.

"Thank you Mr Brown. Your statement will be processed and you will need to sign it. We might have to clarify a few points in a further interview." The Detective Chief Inspector stood up and shook hands with Brad. "You can go now."

Brad felt the cool steady hand of the police officer against his sweat covered palm and shuddered. His gait was a little unsteady as he headed for the door.

"Straight forward enough, don't you think, Harry? Got into a bit of a tizz when I asked if he liked Greenhalgh. Do you think there's something to unearth there?"

"I dunno. He certainly wasn't at ease. But then, he's had a drink or two, and I suppose he's had a fright."

"Pity he hadn't a golfing partner to confirm what he told us."

The significance of his superior's remark wasn't lost on Sergeant Barnes. "Big difference in build. I'd reckon Carlton Greenhalgh could wipe the floor with that wee snout if he tried anything."

"Mmm .... you could be right. We'll have a word with the professional, next. Bring Dougie Watson through, please."

Dougie came in and took over the seat vacated by Bradley Brown and the formalities were completed before the detective embarked on his questioning.

"Can you confirm when you arrived here this morning, Mr Watson?"

"Just after seven-thirty. Graham was already in the shop ahead of me."

"And Graham is?"

"My assistant."

Yates paused to make some notes before resuming. "You remained in the shop all morning until Bradley Brown came to tell you he'd found a body?"

"In, or around."

"Is Mr Brown right in saying he met you outside the shop?"

"Yes. I'd been in the clubhouse to use the loo."

"Can you say how long you were away?"

Dougie felt inclined to say as long as it takes to crap but decided on a little more decorum. "About ten, fifteen minutes, or there-about."

"And did you see Carlton Greenhalgh at any time this morning?"

"Don't think so. Mind I see dozens of golfers. They don't all register. He comes most Sundays. Plays with Nick Baker and Grant Mason. A couple of useful players. Out of his class really."

"So Greenhalgh wasn't a good golfer in your opinion?"

"He thought he was. Too ham-fisted."

"Did you like the man?"

"You didn't like Carlton, he imposed himself on you and you put up with him. He was a pompous arse, in fact."

DCI Yates continued with the questioning and Dougie confirmed Bradley's account of events.

"You were able to identify the body by the golf shoes he was wearing, I believe?"

"They're quite distinctive as I told James Winter."

"What did you do when you were left alone with the body? Did you touch it at all?"

"Not after I tried his wrist for a pulse. I made myself as comfortable on the grass as I could and waited. Brad came over and I told him it was Carlton."

"You didn't see anyone else? Or anything at all unusual?"

"Apart from the odd crow and a rabbit, no. I heard the chap that owns the renovated house facing the eighteenth mowing his lawn."

After a few more questions, Dougie was dismissed.

"Two down and dozens more to go," the DCI said. "Still want to play detective, Harry? Do you think we've advanced any?"

"Not a lot."

"You're wrong. I'm getting a picture of this Greenhalgh fellow. It's like writing a book. You have to get inside your main characters. Now, let's see if James Winter can tell us anything."

James Winter, looking pale and nervous, sat hands clasped to answer the Detective Chief Inspector's queries. Every so often he released them to adjust his glasses. His story ran on the same lines as the two men previously interviewed from the moment Bradley and Dougie had gone into his office with the news. Prior to that, he said he'd reached the club shortly before nine and hadn't left his office. Agnes, the dining manageress, had brought him tea about a quarter after ten o'clock and he hadn't finished drinking it when they delivered the bombshell. When asked if he had seen Carlton Greenhalgh earlier that morning he confirmed he had.

"He was over by the car park when I arrived."

"So you saw him shortly before nine o'clock?"

"That's correct."

"Was he alone?"

"No he was talking to Babs Slater, a lady member. They walked off together towards the practice area."

"Did Mr Greenhalgh often converse with the lady members?"

"He had his favourites."

"And Babs Slater was in that category?"

James Winter blushed, "I believe he was very fond of Babs. He was a married man, of course."

The Detective Chief Inspector shuffled his papers.

"And where precisely is the practice area?"

"Over by the car park. To the right of the eighteenth green. It runs up almost to the seventeenth rough. You can see it from the forecourt."

"And did you see him, or Babs Slater, again?"

"No. Not until I saw his body. It's a terrible tragedy.

Such a distinguished man."

"I gather you liked Mr Greenhalgh?"

"Of course, I did. Carlton was a fine fellow. Did a lot for the club. We were close friends at one time."

"But not recently?"

"Well, you know how it is. He was a little too assured. I think he'd have liked my job. He always wanted to organise things when he was captain. We had our differences, I can't deny it, but I still respected the poor devil, despite everything."

"So there you are, Harry," DCI Yates said when James Winter had left. "The picture changes slightly. We have a different opinion of Carlton and we now know he liked the ladies, or one lady member in particular."

"I see what you mean about building up the picture."

"Good."

The police constable at the lounge door came over and spoke to his superiors. "The victim's son, Edward Greenhalgh, is here and getting restless, Sir. Says he's anxious to go and see his mother, Sir."

"Thank you. We'll see him now."

Detective Chief Inspector Yates stood up as Edward Greenhalgh entered. The son was tall, brown haired, with the suggestion of a moustache above his upper lip. Outwardly, he appeared to control his feelings. His steel grey eyes stared straight at the detective as the latter began questioning.

He was, he said, twenty-six years old and had married last year. He stayed with his wife in a flat five minutes away from his parents' home and continued to see them regularly. He had met his father briefly in the locker room that morning. It would have been about a quarter to eight. His father had told him he had time to kill on the practice area as he wasn't playing with Nick and Grant until ten.

The DCI raised his eyebrows at the words 'time to kill' but Edward Greenhalgh showed no reaction. He told how he'd arranged a game with Grant's son, Dominic for five to eight. They were playing early because Dominic had to be home for his baby's christening at eleven-thirty. He was upset because his father refused to go, being a non-Christian.

Edward Greenhalgh paused as if gathering his thoughts "We reached the fourteenth green, having cut out a couple of holes, before ten, and Dominic left. I stayed on the course to finish the round."

He told the detective he estimated it took him a further forty minutes. He said he was leaving the course without entering the club house and was part way home when he was called by James Winter and it was suggested he return immediately. Winter advised him there had been a serious incident involving his father. On arriving back at the clubhouse, he accompanied the secretary to the table he was sharing with Dougie Watson and Bradley Brown and learned his father had died. He knew no details until the news was released to everyone.

"It must have come as a terrible shock. Please accept our condolences."

Edward nodded and Yates continued.

"Can you recall who was playing in front or behind you?"

"There was a chap on his own a couple of holes back, too far to positively identify him. I thought it might be Bradley Brown because of his high swing, but I wouldn't swear to it. I didn't pay much attention to him. There was no-one immediately ahead."

"And did you see Bradley once you'd come in?"

"No. I went straight to the car park. Like I said, I didn't go into the clubhouse."

"Did you have a good relationship with your father?"

"Not especially. He wasn't an easy man to live with. I was quite pleased to leave home when I married."

"And your mother? Did she appear happy?"

"Mother doesn't appear anything. She gets on with living. My parents are... were... both strong people."

"Did you ever consider your father might be having an affair? Say with Bab's Slater?"

"I knew he buttered her up. An affair's a bit strong."

"And how did you react to this.... buttering up? Did it bother you?"

"It embarrassed me to see them together. They weren't very discreet in and around the clubhouse sometimes."

"Did you speak to him about his behaviour?"

"Of course not. She wasn't the first you know. I don't understand how mother put up with it for so long. She was coming to her senses, though. She told me she was thinking of a divorce. Said she didn't want me to be upset. I told her to go for it. Except perhaps financially, she'd be better off without him." Edward Greenhalgh's manner had become agitated as he spoke. "At least now she won't have to face up to that. Fate's stepped in at the crucial moment."

"It wasn't fate. Mr Greenhalgh. It was murder. Murder is liable to be far more distressing than divorce."

Edward lowered his head. "Of course, it's terrible." For the first time his face crumpled and he'd to wipe away a tear. "Even in death the old man couldn't get it right."

Detective Chief Inspector Yates stood up. "Thank you, Mr Greenhalgh, you are free to go. I may wish to speak to you again."

Sergeant Barnes scratched his head. "Edward Greenhalgh is a cool customer," he observed. "People are complicated. I got the impression his little show of grief was for our benefit."

"And murder is a bum," Yates added.

"What led you to think that Greenhalgh and Ms Slater were romantically linked?"

"Intuition. Pure intuition, Harry. And now, I'm going to leave you for an hour. Take statements from those remaining in the lounge. I believe that includes the men the victim was supposed to play with but keep Babs Slater until I'm back. I'll have a chat with her myself."

"Can I ask where you're going?"

"To take a wander on the golf course. Starting at the fourteenth. Don't work too hard."

CHAPTER 3

It took twelve minutes of comfortable walking for Raymond Yates to reach the fourteenth tee. The layout of the course sent its fairway in the direction of the clubhouse. The short fifteenth and the sixteenth doubled back before the seventeenth and eighteenth headed again towards the nineteenth hole, the name golfers call their clubhouse. He stood taking in the warm summer air. On a day like this, in different circumstances, it would be near paradise.

Yates looked to his left, across the fifteenth and eighteenth holes to the practice area. Any figure playing there would be visible to a golfer on the fourteenth tee. If that figure were familiar, he would be recognised even allowing for the distance. The DCI took out his note book and jotted down his observations. He walked on across the deserted course, not down the fourteenth fairway but skirting the fifteenth green to the slight hollow that housed the last tee. From behind it he glanced up the seventeenth fairway to where the incident van stood almost concealed by trees in the deep rough. Some thirty metres further on near and around the spot where Carlton Greenhalgh's body had lain, his men were still searching for clues. With his back to the clubhouse, the practice area lay immediately to his right. Beyond it, backing on to the course, was the renovated house referred to by Dougie.

Acting on impulse, DCI Yates made his way to its boundary, vaulted a low garden wall and knocked on the open house door. An elderly man in well-worn tweeds answered and Detective Chief Inspector Yates introduced himself.

"I realised there was a bit of a commotion when I saw your men and the police van. Man dead, you say?"

"Afraid so. One witness said he'd heard you mowing the lawn. I don't suppose you saw or heard anything unusual. Someone crying out, perhaps?"

"Hear cries from the course frequently. Shouts of "fore" and the birds. Lots of shrieks and squawks from them. Can't say I was aware of any out of the ordinary noise. The mower's pretty deafening."

"And did you see anyone on the course early this morning?"

"Not on the course, itself. I did see a couple, man and woman. It must have been around half-nine because I was just thinking of starting on the front beds. On a day like this it's great to get out early. But that wasn't unusual. I saw them quite often. Normally, they were having a bit of a canoodle. Stealing the odd kiss in between shots, you could say."

"Were they canoodling, today?"

"No they were talking. And come to think of it, not too friendly, either. She was pushing him about a bit and he appeared to slap her face and storm off."

"Which way did he go?"

"Up towards the end of the practice area. Where it joins the rough. Some of them cut over that way and play in. I feel tempted to do it myself. I live here yet I've to wait at least another year before I can become a member."

"Bad deal. Which way did the woman go?"

"Towards the eighteenth."

"Was the man on the practice area carrying his golf clubs?"

"Just the one, I think. I didn't actually see him go on to the course. I went round the side to my greenhouse. I've some nice pelargonium. Thought I'd put them out in the front border. It took a while to sort them."

"And you saw nothing else?"

"Well, I saw your lot, later. Wait a minute, I believe there was someone else in the rough."

"Can you describe that person?"

"No it was just a fleeting glance. In fact it might have been a bit earlier."

"Can you describe the couple you saw in the practice area?"

"She was quite small with short blonde curly hair. A bit plump. He was pretty tall, maybe, 5ft 11ins and quite broad with it. I don't mean fat. Well built, about my size. He'd on one of those visors and she was wearing red shorts. The kind that go below the knees. He was getting on a bit and I doubt if she's far off forty."

"Thank you Mr.......?

"Martin - Callum Martin-retired Engineer."

"I'll send an officer round to take a full statement from you. Thanks again."

Yates made a more orthodox exit through Mr Martin's gate. He was smiling as he crossed over a track and back into the practice ground, from where he made his way up towards the incident van. Things were moving along merrily.

Constable Thomas sat on the step of the police van. He jumped to attention as Yates approached.

"Any luck?" Yates asked.

"I'd say so, Sir. Reckon we might have the weapon. It was handed in a matter of minutes ago, Sir. I've notified Sergeant Barnes. He said you were out on the course, Sir."

"Great! Had a feeling it wouldn't be far away. A golf club?"

"Yes, Sir. Five iron. MacGregor. It was in the ditch this side of the eighteenth tee, Sir. Looks as though it's been cleaned, but there are some traces we think are blood, Sir. It's inside."

Detective Chief Inspector Yates went into the van. The golf club had been placed in a clear polythene exhibit bag and was lying on the table with a few other items. He picked it up and examined it. "Wouldn't be surprised if this is what we're looking for. Can't be many good clubs thrown into ditches."

"Whoever discarded it must be daft, Sir. We were bound to find it. Shouldn't take long to establish who's missing a MacGregor five iron."

"Not long at all, Constable. I think I already know."

"You do, Sir?" Constable Thomas looked incredulously at his superior, who merely grinned back.

"So what else have we?" DCI Yates asked.

"The usual buttons, cigarette ends, a few tatty golf balls and a mass of footprints. Most showing stud marks."

The detective scanned through the selection of polythene bags on the table. "Think I'll call the boys in Thomas. You can tell them and then go and get a signed statement from Callum Martin. He's the chap that lives in the house by the eighteenth. You can use my notes." Yates removed a sheet from his pad and handed it to P C Thomas. "Should this club prove not to be our weapon, we can resume the search. The area's to remain cordoned and a couple of men will be designated to stay here with the van. I'll arrange for the exhibits to be collected and sent to the labs at once. Well done."

DCI Yates went back to the clubhouse and made straight for the male locker room. The walls of the room were lined with long narrow cupboards suitable for taking a bag of clubs. Below them were benches, beneath which shelves housed shoes and holdalls. A further row of lockers ran down the centre of the room and each individual locker was numbered. A large notice board near the door gave information of competitions, prize winners and events, and a variety of lists. Among the latter, he found one headed 'LOCKERS'. It detailed the names of members and beside each was a number. Yates ran his finger down the names until he came to Carlton Greenhalgh - 45.

Locker 45, he discovered, was firmly padlocked. He took a penknife from his pocket and forced the lock with the skill of someone who had done the same task many times before. The locker opened to reveal a bag full of clubs, an umbrella, gloves and packs of Pinnacle balls. It took a fraction of a second to see the clubs were MacGregor's and the No 5 iron was missing.

It had been easy for the Detective Chief Inspector to break into the locker, but it took several minutes for him to secure it again. For added measure he took a roll of police security tape from his pocket and formed a huge cross with it, doubly sealing the locker. He made a note in his book for the clubs to be picked up and removed to the station, then went through to the family lounge where Sergeant Barnes was dismissing a lady member.

"As I said to your sergeant. He was a lovely man. I

knew when he was late this morning there had to be something wrong. Carlton was always punctual." With a sniff into her tissue, the woman left to join her friend, who had already said her piece to the sergeant.

"Who was that?" The DCI asked.

"Marion Chapman. She and her friend, Philippa Goldsmith, went ahead of Greenhalgh's playing partners when he failed to keep to his tee off time." Sergeant Barnes tidied up a pile of notes. "Glad you're back. I've got through most of the interviews except the staff and Babs Slater. She's decidedly lonely out there. Her lady partner had to be away sharp, so I saw her first. It probably looked a bit obvious, leaving Babs till last."

"Well, someone has to be at the end of the line. How did Bradley Brown get home? He'd had a few drinks."

"He wasn't the only one. Their wives came to the rescue. Bradley got a lift from a Nick Baker. We've had the local reporter at the door and the Dailies have been on the phone. I was brief. Told them a man's body had been found on the course and that a further report would follow when we knew more. I didn't give the name of the victim or anything in case some of his relatives don't know yet."

"Very wise. Anything else interesting to report?"

"The men think they've got the weapon..."

The DCI interrupted, "I know. I've inspected it. The club they found belongs to Carlton Greenhalgh. I broke into his locker and checked."

"Whew! You don't waste time, Sir. How was your walk?"

"Revealing." Yates ran through what he had learned from Mr Martin.

"Do you think she could have done it?"

"It's possible but improbable. What about the interviews?

Anything?"

"Pretty dull and unproductive. The two chaps he was due to play with carried on

without him when he didn't turn up. They seem to know very little. But they did confirm what young Graham Livesay had to tell us, though."

"What was that?"

"They saw Babs Slater go into the shop about ten to ten. Graham says she took Dougie into a corner away from the counter and seemed agitated. Unfortunately, the phone rang and Graham had to go into the back shop to answer it. She was away when he came out and then Dougie excused himself. Said he was going to the toilet. I've got it all down."

"Good. We'll go over it later. Let's put Babs out of her misery."

"Take more than us to do that, I'm afraid. She's been sobbing all afternoon."

***

"Would you like a cup of tea, Mrs Slater?" Detective Chief Inspector Yates employed his softest manner. "I was about to order one for the Sergeant and myself."

Babs Slater nodded her curly head in acceptance.

Sergeant Barnes was reminded of photographs he'd seen in his mother's collection of Shirley Temple as a kid. Babs had a round childish face with dimples on either cheek. At that moment, it was distorted as she fought to stem the flow of tears. Her nose and eyes were red and her make up streaked on to her cheeks. Normally, he supposed she was quite a pretty woman. Small, soft blonde curls and rather too full curves but, nevertheless, curves. Not the type you'd expect to wield a golf club. Yet she was considered a good player if you believed Marion Chapman's statement. The tea came on a tray brought by Constable Pauline Fergus, who had been drafted to assist, and the steward's wife, Sheenagh, had included chocolate biscuits. Detective Chief Inspector Yates filled the cups himself and bit into a Kit-Kat.

"We're sorry to have kept you waiting. I see from the sheet you arrived at the golf club this morning at eight-thirty. Was it customary for you to be so early?"

"It varied. But Sundays I usually go to the practice ground before playing in the medal. It's our alternative day - the day set aside for those who work and can't play Wednesdays, the normal medal day. I'm a hairdresser, part time."

"And you were playing in the medal, today?"

"No, as it happens. Most of the good players were at the Laureston Open Day. It was over-subscribed and I didn't get a place, so I decided to have a game with a friend, Muriel Saunders, rather than wait for the ladies' ballot at twelve-thirty. It was such a lovely day." Babs punctuated every sentence with sobs and sniffles.

"But you still came early to practice. Any particular reason why?"

"No. Not really."

"So what time did you tee off?"

"We didn't. Muriel couldn't make an early time. We were next to go out when we were told the course had been closed until further notice, and we were all made to go into the dining lounge. There were so many rumours. We realised something awful had happened because the ambulance and the police arrived."

"When did you find out Carlton Greenhalgh had been killed?"

"When you told us."

"And you knew nothing of it before?"

"No. How could I? We were in here the whole time."

"Right, now let's go back to when you arrived at the course at, you say, eight-thirty. What did you do then?"

"I got my trolley from the lock-up in the car park and left it round the side while I fetched my clubs from my locker and changed into my golf shoes and things."

"Were any other ladies about at that time?"

"No. I saw Marion Chapman and Philippa Goldsmith on the first tee, later, when I was in having a coffee, but I hadn't spoken to them."

"Did they see you?"

"I doubt it. They were teeing off and I was in the lounge."

"Once you'd changed into your shoes etc., where did you go?"

"I took the clubs to my trolley and went to the practice area."

"Did you see anyone?"

Babs burst into even deeper sobs before answering. "I bumped into Carlton. He was going to practice. And James Winter, the secretary, drove up. There were one or two other players in the car park. I'm not sure who they were."

"Can you recall what time that would be?"

"Ten to nine, perhaps."

"I would like you to answer me carefully, Mrs Slater."

"I prefer Miss Slater. Slater's my maiden name," Babs interrupted. "I reverted to it after my divorce."

"Thank you for putting me right. As I said, please think carefully before you answer this question. Had you arranged to meet Carlton Greenhalgh on the practice area?"

Babs looked up as if surprised. "No. I had not."

"But you were accustomed to meeting him there?"

"We sometimes practiced at the same time."

"I believe you partnered Mr Greenhalgh in some tournaments?"

"That's right. In mixed competitions."

"So you got on well together?"

"Yes."

"Again, I must ask you to answer carefully. Was there more to your relationship with Mr Greenhalgh other than as golf partners?"

Babs Slater kept her head down as she replied. "We were very good friends."

"I put it to you that you and Carlton Greenhalgh were deeply involved with each other. That, in fact, you were lovers."

Babs Slater didn't answer. She couldn't. She broke down in a flood of tears. Detective Chief Inspector Yates waited patiently for her to recover. "More tea?" he asked, when she finally quietened, and she accepted.

Her hands shook as she picked up the cup and sipped the drink.

"I realise this must be very painful to you, but I have a job to do and that involves finding out as much as I can about Carlton Greenhalgh in order to elucidate who killed him and why. I'm sure you want to help."

The blonde head nodded.

"I'll ask you once more. Had you arranged to meet Mr Greenhalgh on the practice area this morning?"

"Yes," she replied, sheepishly.

"Who made the arrangement? You, or Carlton?"

"He did."

"And was it for any particular reason?"

"No we often met there. We usually had the place to ourselves."

"And you were alone this morning?"

"Yes."

"And did Carlton seem his normal self?"

"Yes."

"Then can you explain to me why a witness says he saw you apparently arguing? That you were pushing Carlton about and that he appeared to storm off?"

Babs Slater gasped audibly. "It wasn't like that."

"Wasn't it? Then what was it like?"

Babs paused for a full thirty seconds before saying, "He was being difficult. I wanted him to leave his wife to live at my place. He said he couldn't yet. That's all it was. I got upset and he went off to play down the eighteenth."

Yates consulted his note book. "I believe you knew Carlton Greenhalgh a long time ago. When you lived here as a child, in fact."

"I knew his younger brother, Kevin. He's in Australia, now. We were friends at school."

"But you also knew Carlton didn't you?"

"Yes."

"Did you go out with him?"

"I was just a young girl. Sixteen. He was years older. He took me out once or twice. My mother didn't approve. Then I went to live with my Aunt May in Sussex."

"So when you came back to Fisborough .... what was it eighteen months ago....... you resumed your friendship?"

"I met up with him when I joined the golf club and we became golfing partners. Then it sort of grew into more. We went to the hotel in Laureston for drinks and to eat sometimes. Have you met his wife? She's a cold woman. I know they all say it, but she really didn't understand him."

"So it's your belief Carlton and his wife didn't have a happy marriage?"

"They didn't have a marriage."

"Were you in love with Carlton Greenhalgh?"

"I loved him, in a way. More than she did, anyhow."

"What about his son? Do you know if he got on with him?"

"Edward? He didn't say much about him. They didn't seem to do anything together like father and son. I've never known them to play golf with each other, for instance."

"Do you have a family?"

Babs answered the question calmly. "I had a son. Before I was married. He was adopted. I couldn't have any more."

"Do you live alone?"

"Yes, I divorced eight years ago. I took over my mother's house when she died. It's not big but it is mine."

"Do you know of anyone who might have wanted Carlton dead?"

"No, he was a popular, well-liked man."

"Thank you. You've been very helpful. We'll leave it at that. I will, however, have to speak to you again. Do you have anyone to drive you home?"

"I'll be all right. It's not far."

"I'll arrange for a constable to take you in your own car. I think you should get some rest."

Babs got to her feet, shook hands and left with Gregg Thomas.

"I must be getting soft, Harry," Raymond Yates said as they prepared to leave the golf club.

"Don't know about that. Do you believe what she says about what happened at the practice area?"

"At this stage, I believe very little anyone tells me until I can prove it. We'll question the staff sometime tomorrow. Hand over those notes and I'll take them to bed with me tonight."

"You're not married then?"

Raymond Yates grinned. "Who'd marry a cop?"

"Mary did. She's my missus. I married a saint."

"Well, Harry, I doubt if there are many Saint Mary's around but I'll keep looking. We've met the girl friend, now it's time to meet the wife.

Sergeant Barnes looked into the lounge before he left.

"Could you keep that room available for us to use tomorrow?" he asked the club steward, Jack Davis, indicating the family room.

"We've no functions booked for a couple of days. Should be all right. How're the inquiries progressing?"

"We'll get there," the sergeant said.

"If you need a bit of insight into some of the members, ask my wife, Sheenagh. What she doesn't know, no-one knows."

"Thanks. I'll bear that in mind."

***

Detective Chief Inspector Yates opted to take his BMW and Sergeant Barnes climbed into the passenger seat, relieved his driving skills weren't under scrutiny. Superior officers, even plain clothes ones, made him feel inferior no matter how good he was at something. Yates, he conceded, could prove the exception.

The two police officers reached Montgomery Square where Greenhalgh had lived with his wife, Elizabeth.

"Very desirable residences, wouldn't you say, Harry?" the Chief observed.

"If you mean posh," Sergeant Barnes replied. "I agree. Now, which is number 19?"

They had little difficulty locating it. At first glance all the houses were identical, red sandstone, detached villas but a second inspection showed that No 19 was a double integral garage larger, a wrought iron gate wider and it boasted a distinguishable extra external light with flashing alarm system.

"Anything you can do, we can do better," DCI Yates sung as they opened the gate and rung a melodic door bell.

The door was opened by one of the women police constables he'd sent to inform Mrs Greenhalgh of her husband's demise. The detectives were shown into an opulently furnished lounge where Carlton's wife rose from her chair to greet them.

In contrast to Babs Slater, Elizabeth was tall, elegantly dressed in a simple bottle green skirt and jumper which suited her light olive complexion. Her, probably tinted, reddish brown hair, was neatly clasped in a chignon. She was not a beautiful woman. Her features were too sharp, her grey eyes and lips too thin but, for her fifty-six years, some would say she was well preserved. There was, however, an aloofness about her and although her expression was serious, she was composed and gave no outward sign of grieving.

Yates extended his sympathy to the woman and she accepted his remarks calmly.

"Please," she said, "Let's be seated."

Harry Barnes was reminded of the vicar speaking after prayers on Sunday morning at St Peter's. A service he'd been quite happy to miss in the line of duty. No doubt, Mary had gone as usual.

In reply to the Chief's questions, Elizabeth Greenhalgh explained she had seen her husband briefly that morning at breakfast. He had been in his usual rush to get to the golf course, and, no, he hadn't appeared to have anything else on his mind. He was away by eight and had said he'd be back about four-thirty but would phone if he was staying on to play bridge. He did that sometimes.

"And what did you do this morning?"

"I went to see a friend, Sally Cornwell. She has a market garden and we had coffee and sandwiches together on her terrace."

The detective noted the name and address of her friend.

"At what time would that be?"

"I must have got there between half ten and a quarter to eleven, I suppose."

"And you left at ...?"

"When Julia, she's a student who does a spot of cleaning for me at weekends, phoned to say two police officers had turned up and wanted to speak to me urgently. I didn't know what had happened until I arrived here and was told."

"You must have been very shocked?"

"Of course, I don't think I've taken it in yet."

"Were you anywhere in the vicinity of the club earlier this morning?"

"I had no need to be."

"So between the time your husband left until you went to Sally Cornwall's sometime after ten o'clock, you were on your own in the house?"

"That's right. Julia has a key. She was due to arrive about half ten."

"Am I to understand Marion Chapman was mistaken when she says in her statement that she saw you there?"

"She has to be if that's what she said."

Yates looked at her closely and she returned his gaze. He changed the direction of his questioning.

"Do you know if your husband had any problems?"

"Carlton always had problems of a sort. Being the Chief Sales and Marketing man for Hobson and Cartridge was a very responsible position. Outside work, I don't believe so."

"Were you aware if your husband had any enemies? Anyone who might bear him a grudge?"

"Enemies? I'm afraid I can't help you there. I didn't know many of his friends or acquaintances. They revolved mostly around the business and golf and bridge."

"Are you a member of the Golf Club?"

Elizabeth Greenhalgh gave a cynical laugh, "Me, a member of the club? I'm the Lady Vice Captain."

"I see. You'll appreciate it's my job to ask difficult questions. Would you say you and your husband enjoyed a happy relationship?"

"It worked for the most part. We had a pleasant, comfortable, life style. No money worries, or anything."

"And your intimate life was satisfactory?"

"You must understand, we were past romance. We've had separate rooms for a long time but the doors weren't locked."

"Did you ever suspect your husband of seeing someone else?"

Elizabeth Greenhalgh visibly stiffened. "Carlton thrived on affairs. Most of them short-lived. There have been other women in our marriage since the start. But it was me he was married to, not them. He had his flings but we remained a couple. Thirty-two years in September since we married. That's a very long time. We had a loose relationship on both sides. No tightly knotted strings."

"So you weren't jealous?"

Elizabeth Greenhalgh paused before confessing, "If I'm to be honest, I guess I was at first, but you're the only person I've admitted it to."

"And was Carlton to your knowledge currently involved with someone?"

"You're bound to find out if you haven't already - Babs Slater. She's probably weeping like a baby at this moment."

"And what did you think about their relationship?"

"It wouldn't have lasted long. She was always pestering him. Ringing him up. I asked him to tell her to stop and he said she was a silly bitch and indicated he would speak to her. He said she was nothing more than a cursed nuisance. Apparently they were friends years ago and she left the area. She tried to pick up with him again recently when she returned after her mother died."

"And had he spoken to her?"

"I wouldn't think he'd had time. We only talked last night. Carlton was well liked at the club, you know. He certainly enjoyed his golf."

Having successfully turned the questioning away from Babs Slater, Elizabeth Greenhalgh answered the DCI's final queries confidently enough.

***

"The victim's wife .... what did you make of her, Harry?"

"She's controlled. Comes over as a bit hard, I'd say."

"Yes. You can see why he philandered. She says they had a loose relationship. My guess is she'd have had him in a straight jacket if he'd been a weaker man. I think our Elizabeth is quite a prickly character and I don't think she told us everything. I got the impression she was holding back. And she has no one to verify she was at home during the vital period between nine and ten."

"We could try to check it out with the neighbours. They might have seen her."

"I think we'll call it a day. I want to go over what we've got so far. You can do the same and we'll meet up at the station in the morning. You can leave your uniform in the wardrobe. You'll be joining me in the plain clothes division, Harry. So where is it you live? I'll drop you off."

"My car's still at Fisborough Golf Club. Perhaps you could take me back there?"

"Fisborough it is."

Harry Barnes bade farewell to Yates at the entrance to the Golf Club and drove home to his cosy nest. Mary had baked ham in an orange sauce set on a mixed salad, topped with onion rings. It tasted heavenly.

CHAPTER 4

Sergeant Barnes arrived on duty next morning, a good fifteen minutes before he was due in, to find Detective Chief Inspector Yates already making notes.

"I couldn't sleep for the sun pouring in through my bedroom window and thought I'd make an early start," the latter explained. "I've worked out a schedule and I rang the course and said play can resume as long as no-one crosses the cordons. There are a couple of our men supervising the area. I reckon we should pay another visit to the Greenhalgh residence. I've a search warrant in case his wife objects to us going through his stuff. After that, we'll probably make for the course and have a word with the staff."

"What about this station? There's normally just four of us and that isn't always enough."

"I've asked headquarters to lend you a couple of men, both experienced Detective Constables. Do you know Harvey and Jacobs?"

"I've met them."

"Constable Thomas and WPC Pauline Fergus," Raymond Yates smiled at the young policewoman, attractive in her spanking new uniform, "will cope until they get here. Any emergencies and they can use the mobiles. Let's go and surprise Mrs Greenhalgh."

"I take it she doesn't know we're coming, then? Isn't eight in the morning a bit larkish. Might catch her in the shower."

"Wouldn't that be something? You know what they say about the early bird? You're looking very dapper, Harry, I didn't say it had to be Sunday best." The DCI quipped. After one day working together a friendly rapport was developing between the two men.

"Suit I got for my niece's twenty-first. She'd a party at Bonnington's. Collar and tie affair, until it warmed up and everyone discarded jackets and rolled their shirt sleeves up for a cha-cha."

"Right, let's get on our way. It's your turn to drive."

With the roles reversed, Harry Barnes was relieved he reached Montgomery Square without incident. A few neighbours were setting off for work and the police car attracted the attention of some of them.

"Do you suppose she's told anyone what's happened, Sir."

"Who knows but news like murder spreads quickly. And remember no need for the title, unless we're in company."

"Yes, Sir ... I mean ..."

Yates laughed but his face was serious as he rang the bell. The door was opened almost immediately by Elizabeth. No towelling bathrobe, hair curlers or face pack. This woman was up, smartly suited, and ready to go somewhere. She drew back as she recognised the figures on the doorstep.

"Oh. It's you."

"Were you expecting someone else?"

"Yes. My son, Edward. We're going into the city. I've an appointment with my solicitor."

"Don't worry about us." The Detective Chief Inspector

was already stepping past her into the hall. Sergeant Barnes followed. "We'll make sure the house is secure when we leave." He sensed Elizabeth Greenhalgh was about to protest and added. "It's important we look through your late husband's personal papers and so on. It's essential to the investigation and we do have a warrant. I can assure you we will be as careful as possible."

Edward appeared at the open door. "Mother, are you......?" He saw the police officers. "So it's your car outside? I did wonder."

"We've a warrant to go through your father's papers etc. Anything that might shed light on his murder, you understand?"

"It's not very convenient this morning. Couldn't you come another time?"

"We've a very busy schedule, Mr Greenhalgh, and are quite happy to lock the house up securely. I promise you, your mother won't know we've been here."

"It's all right," Elizabeth sighed. "They can't do much harm. Carlton's bedroom's front right. His desk is in the morning room. That's the small room at the back of the house. All his things are in those two rooms. To set the alarm when you leave you'll find the code listed on the inside of the cupboard door above the refrigerator. The spare house key's there, too. Just drop it through the letter box once you've locked up, and be careful. Now, please excuse us." Mother and son left. The imminent departure of the city train proving too big a pull.

The officers decided to start at the top and work down. Carlton's room was the least imposing of the four bedrooms. It was furnished with a simple, single divan bed, a double wardrobe and a chest of drawers. A small fitted vanity unit, comprising wash hand basin, towel rail and shelved cupboard, housed his electric razor, after shave and vitamin pills. Above it a bevelled mirror reflected the painting of a semi-nude girl which was on the wall beside his bed. All in good taste, Yates thought, admiring the brushwork of the artist.

The room was meticulously tidy. A full length mirror lined the back of the bedroom door. The walls were plain white emulsion.

"Start on the dressing chest, Harry. I'll tackle the wardrobe."

They set to work. Harry lifted the items from each drawer and checked there was nothing hidden, while the DCI fingered his way through the pockets of suits, trousers, jackets and overcoats. The lack of any clutter made the task easy.

"Nothing of any obvious interest to us here," Harry said. "Have you come up with anything?"

"Not even a jelly baby."

The vanity unit surrendered a couple of packets of condoms. Yates waved them in the air. "Not for Elizabeth's benefit, I bet," he laughed.

"Wonder how long they've had separate rooms. Odd how some folk live." Harry thought of the king sized double he shared with Mary.

"Maybe, he snored."

"That'll be right. Is that us finished in here?"

"Not quite." The DCI went over to the bed and lifted the overlay and quilt. "Thought as much," he said as he revealed two drawers in the base of the bed. The first contained bed linen and spare towels. The second a pile of magazines. Yates lifted them out on to the bed. "Our victim liked his bedtime reading," he said as he flicked through the mildly pornographic literature. "Pretty tame. You can buy this stuff in any newsagent's." Harry blinked at a revealing picture of a girl in nothing but a suspender belt and black stockings. "Says something about the man, though, doesn't it?" his Chief added.

"Yet he had his girlfriend."

"Yes, but possibly not when he needed her. Hold on a minute. What's this?"

From the pages of the last magazine an opened envelope fell on to the bed cover. Yates took out the folded sheet inside. Harry came across and read over his shoulder a note written on Fisborough Golf Club headed paper.

Dear Carlton,

You are the last person I would choose to ask but things are a bit desperate. I need at least £1000. I think this money is due after all this time.

Perhaps, you could discuss it with me in private at the club as soon as possible.

The note was dated 30th July and signed - Dougie Watson.

"Short and sweet and to the point, eh?" Yates observed, putting the note into his document case.

"Blackmail?"

"Isn't threatening enough. The plot deepens. It certainly opens up a new aspect. Time we moved on."

Elizabeth Greenhalgh's room was larger and had an en-suite toilet and shower. Here the emulsion was tinged lilac and the cornices of the ceiling were depicted in a deeper shade of mauve. The room was more sumptuously furnished, and every bit as tidy, as her husband's. Her bed was a large double with ornately carved headboard. She had fitted wardrobes, displaying an expensive taste in classic clothes and enough shoes to fill a Clarke's High Street store. She also had a fine array of perfumes.

"Funny," Yates said, "I always equate perfume with passion."

"Well, it's the exception proves the rule. No sign of Carlton having been in here recently," Harry said, pulling back the pillows to reveal a lonely satin nightdress.

They found little of interest in Elizabeth Greenhalgh's room or either of the guest's rooms, apart from a photograph of Grant Mason in Elizabeth's bedside drawer.

"Odd," Yates commented, showing it to his Sergeant. "Wonder if there's anything to draw from that?"

Downstairs, Carlton's desk sported a Dell Computer and a printer.

"We'll take the machine in. Could be something on the hard drive. We'll get Pauline Fergus or Greg Thomas to run through it. He might even have replied to Dougie. He's had time. This is the 3rd."

The desk drawers gave up share certificates, an insurance policy on his life, another on the house and contents and a T V Licence. There were various business papers which reminded the DCI to call in on Carlton's firm.

"We could fit in a visit to Hobson and Cartridge before we go back to the golf club. They've a branch in Laureston and these suggest he was based there. Don't see a will. Wouldn't mind betting it's on the way to the city with Elizabeth and Edward."

The two officers completed their search and the Dell was safely transported to the car. They spent several minutes checking they had fulfilled their promise to leave things as they found them, before the Chief scribbled a note explaining the removal of the computer and attached a receipt to it. They found the key and secured the house before driving off in the direction of Laureston.

"Just after eleven-fifteen. We'll have a quick word with his colleagues and make tracks to Fisborough Golf Club in time for one of Sheenagh"'s lunch time specials. It's been an interesting morning so far." Satisfaction showed in the detective's voice.

The glass doors of Hobson and Cartridge closed behind the policemen as they entered the brass plated premises in the town's Main Street. An efficient looking receptionist conveyed their business to the senior director and they were shown into his office.

"Felix Kerr. What can I do for you, gentlemen? It's a very sorry business. We heard late yesterday afternoon. Carlton will be a hard man to replace although he was due to retire in a few years."

The discussion with Mr Kerr showed Carlton Greenhalgh to be a highly respected member of the company.

"He had been with us for thirty- five years. Joined as a young man. It was mainly typewriters and duplicators in those days. Today, the majority of our sales are computer packages. Carlton was responsible for both the home and overseas division, though recently he often delegated the travel side."

"Were you aware of his having any business or financial problems?"

"Nothing Carlton couldn't handle. He certainly hadn't any money related difficulties, I'm sure of that. In fact, he recently received a bonus of nearly £50,000. We're really going to miss the fellow. Don't suppose they've been able to arrange a funeral yet? I've a busy week ahead."

"Sorry. I can't help you on that. His body won't be released till our experts have finished with it."

"Quite so. I'll keep in touch with Mrs G, though I don't

like to bother her at this time."

"A fairly fruitless exercise that one," Sergeant Barnes said as they set off for lunch.

"Don't be so negative. Nothing's wasted. We're still filling in that picture. We know the guy was genuinely loaded. That could be a motive in itself. He seems to have left different impressions on people. A Gemini figure, some seem to love and others hate. At least he arouses feelings. Had any further thoughts on Dougie's letter?"

"Maybe, he owed him for something. I did wonder why he had it hidden in that magazine under his bed."

"Yes, gives it greater import. The wording's got me puzzled. I'll tackle Dougie if he's there this afternoon. I expect that young man will come up with something logical. We've just passed Greenhalgh's bank. Pull over and I'll double check his finances. You can stay with the car."

It took no more than five minutes for Yates to return. "Smarmy chap that Bank Manager. He didn't give much away. Carlton's as sound as a bell though. In fact he was due to go in and discuss investments this week."

The country road leading to the golf course was, as predicted by Dougie, busier than usual. Several vehicles were parked with their occupants still seated in them and the odd camera was whirring.

"Murder always brings out the gapers. Wonder what they expect to see," the DCI said as they rounded a couple of cars and drove into the parking lot.

The dining lounge had a smattering of women and elderly men gossiping over lunch and coffee.

"The Monday regulars, I guess. I can't think of a better way to spend my days when I retire," the Chief commented.

Agnes brought them the menu in the privacy of the family room, still curtained and out of bounds to members.

"I fancy the cod, Harry. It's on special."

"Cod will suit me fine."

They ordered. "Will you warn Jack and Sheenagh Davis I'd like a word with them when we've eaten, and after, we'll need to see you and Josie, isn't it?" The DCI smiled at Agnes's assistant who appeared somewhat over-awed. "I promise we won't bite your head off."

The fish and chips came with a side salad and lived up to Sheenagh's reputation for producing good food. It was washed down with tea from a large aluminium pot.

"Are you ready for them? Then see if Jack's free?"

Sergeant Barnes walked through to the lounge where Jack was helping behind the bar.

"Okay to come through, Jack?" he asked.

The steward wiped his hands on a towel and preceded the police officer into the family room.

"I expect you get to know the members well?" Yates began.

"Most of them. Of course, there are some as never come in."

"How well did you know Carlton Greenhalgh?"

"He's been a member for years. A regular. Several evenings and always on a Sunday. He's a past captain."

"Well liked, I suppose?"

Jack hesitated. "You had to understand the man. He was a bit pushy. There were those who got on with him, and those who didn't."

"Did you like him?"

"Fair enough."

"And other members of the staff? James Winter, for instance?"

"Those two weren't so pally, lately. But I don't think there was any real trouble. They were quite civil."

"And what about Dougie?"

"Dougie? He's only been here a few months. Doubt if they'd had much contact other than to book tee off times and unless Carlton needed something from the shop."

"I gather Carlton was a man for the ladies?"

"He did chat them up a bit. He was a 'God's gift to women' type."

"Babs Slater?"

"He fancied Babs, I'd say. She's a nice woman."

"You hadn't noticed them drifting apart at all?"

"No they were in here Friday as close as ever. Mind you, she looked out of sorts yesterday morning early on when she was having a coffee with Muriel Saunders. Nothing like what she looked when she heard about Carlton, though."

"And the son?"

"He's a bit stand-offish. Rarely saw him with Carlton. Rumour has it he's inclined to be a tad difficult if his game's not up to scratch. His mother's the same. She came in here, of course, but she hadn't much to say to us."

"Yesterday morning I take it you were here all the time?"

"That's right. Started at seven and had hardly the time to go for a pee."

"You didn't see anything suspicious or unusual? No strangers about?"

"No."

"Thank you, Mr Davis. You've been very helpful."

Sheenagh's evidence was much the same when she was called into the family room. She added a little spice to Carlton's relationship with Babs.

"All over her, he was when he got the chance. Dougie? He seems, okay. Assured like most young men, today."

She had, she said, seen him talking to Babs Slater once or twice. They appeared to be quite friendly, but Babs was friendly with most folk. She could not recall having seen him talking to Carlton. The latter was, she added, too full of himself.

"He was the same in his young days. He married Elizabeth, she came from Petworth, and it made no difference. I've known him since he was a boy. Mind you I was more of an age with Babs."

"You knew Babs Slater when she lived here previously?"

"I was a year above her in the secondary. She was a bright girl. Most thought she'd go on to college but she left quite abruptly to live with her aunt somewhere or other. I'm not one to gossip, but rumour had it she was expecting. In fact, we had a bit of a laugh trying to decide who the father was. Whoops! Sorry. There I go nattering on."

"Please, continue. I find it most interesting," Yates put on his most engaging smile.

"Well, if you're sure. It's all over twenty-five years ago. Babs will be forty odd now and she was barely fifteen then. Can hardly believe how time flies. We thought it might be Kevin's, Carlton's young brother, but it could be Bradley's. He had the hots for her even in those days."

Detective Chief Inspector Yates's ears pricked. "Would that be Bradley Brown?"

"Can't think of any other. He was born in this area and I expect he'll die here. Like myself."

"So at the time Babs left it was considered she could be pregnant by Bradley?"

"He was just one of several. It's all conjecture. We didn't even know for sure she was expecting. But if she was, I'd say it was Kevin's. Bradley would be the long shot. Bab's has never talked about it. Yes, Kevin, and Carlton for that matter, seemed keen on Babs. Kevin was never sporty. He trained as a butcher. Left Fisborough ages ago."

Sheenagh Davis gossiped on but added nothing else to excite the police officers. DCI Yates thanked her and was in the end quite glad to dismiss her.

"Wow! Things are getting more and more interesting, don't you think, Harry?"

"Wow, indeed. Babs said she'd had a baby who was adopted. It all fits. What if that child was Bradley's?"

"Or Carlton's, even? Remember she went out with him, too."

"My God, Sir. You're right. Just supposing she had a child by Carlton."

"We have some research to do, Harry. And it's a delicate matter. Better see the rest of the staff first."

Agnes and Josie were like scared rabbits throughout their interviews and all that was gleaned was that Carlton was generous with his tips and had a passion for strawberry cheese cake and that Elizabeth and Edward were not very popular. Agnes said Carlton enjoyed his whisky but she'd never seen him the worse for drink. She quite liked him and sympathised with him. He was obviously smitten by Babs. It was a shame they couldn't get together.

"So where do we go from here?" The DCI asked when the questioning was completed. "I think we'd better have a resume session. Try and put relevant details together. But you should read this first. It's from Simon Matheson and there's a lab report too."

Harry Barnes read the doctor's note on Carlton Greenhalgh first. Death was estimated between 9.30 and 10.30. It was possible to pin it down to an hour because the body was found so quickly. Cause of death was a heavy blow, in keeping with the plane of a golf swing, to the back of the head. A further two wounds were inflicted when the victim was already grounded. The head of the golf club recovered from the ditch fitted the depressions made on the victim's skull. Traces of blood on the club head were of the same group as Carlton Greenhalgh. It could be taken as conclusive that the golf club was the weapon used to inflict the injuries that led to the death.'

The brief laboratory report confirmed this conclusion. Attempts to get any creditable finger prints from the club had proved impossible.

"That's settled, then. We know that he was killed by his own club. Pity about the prints. Most golfers wear a left hand glove, of course, and the right hand grips over the top, but I was hopeful of at least a right hand thumb print. Have you anything else?"

"There's just one more thing. PC Thomas got the statement from Callum Martin. And he's attached it to your notes." Sergeant Barnes handed over the documents.

"Good man." The detective read through the statement. "Exactly what I wanted. I think you should get back to your station for a while, Harry. I'll try to collate the facts as we now have them. If you've time you could do the same, then we can compare notes. I'll ring you later to make arrangements about tomorrow."

Detective Chief Inspector Yates took his folders and note pads outside to the patio in front of the practice green and the first tee. He sat on a green plastic seat at a green plastic table. Above, a dark blue parasol protected him from the rays of August sunshine. He watched a pair of golfers tee off and wished he could join them. He noted the club flag hanging at half mast, limp in the still air, an honour afforded to all club members. He turned his attention to a fresh note book, dated the page and wrote GREENHALGH CASE.

Methodically he listed all the information seen to be of importance. With that done he began to look at motives. At the end of an hour and a half's deliberations he wrote down six names under the heading main suspects. He also wrote a list of 'still possibles' and one of 'highly unlikelys'. He closed his note book and looked along the patio to the Professional's shop. This, he thought, was as good a time as any to have another talk with Dougie Watson.

Dougie was alone in the shop. He looked up from fitting a new grip on to a putter.

"Good afternoon. Are you needing a set of clubs?"

The DCI smiled back, "Probably. I haven't looked at mine for a while."

"I could fix you a game if you want?"

"Hopefully I'll take you up on that offer soon. Meanwhile, I've to work. I'd like another chat, Dougie. Any chance you could make it now?"

"If you don't want interruptions, I'll have to shut the shop. It's Graham's day off. Should be okay. It's pretty quiet at this time. We get busy again when they start coming down after work."

He followed Yates through the patio doors into the lounge.

"Would you like anything?" DCI Yates asked as they passed the bar.

"A coke would be nice."

"Why not?" Yates ordered one for himself as well and they went into the cool privacy of the curtained family room and seated themselves.

"So what do you need to ask me?" Dougie enquired, apparently relaxed.

"Is there anything else you wish to add to what you've already told us?"

"I don't think so."

"Okay, I thought I'd give you the chance. Something

cropped up when we were going through Carlton Greenhalgh's papers. A letter signed by you requesting a sum of money."

"Oh, that. He owed it to me."

"For what?"

"It's personal."

"I'm afraid in investigating a murder there is nothing too personal. I ask you again – for what?"

"Purchases he made."

"That wasn't the impression I gained from your letter. You have corroboration of these purchases?"

"I might have,"

"I will need to see it."

"And I'm not prepared to go into detail about it. To me, personal means personal. It's not as if I've been arrested or anything. I'm not under oath."

"No, but withholding evidence can be a criminal offence."

"I've done nothing wrong. I'm not a murderer."

With that Dougie got up and returned to his shop.

"Let's hope he doesn't regret this," Yates said under his breath.

PC Greg Thomas, who had been on duty at the incident van, came into the family lounge.

"Good morning Sir. Whoops! It's afternoon, sorry. I heard you were here. Nothing else of any significance has been gained from the search. Do you want us to stay on site?"

"It's not a bad idea to retain a presence. Someone might come in with new evidence. You never know."

"Right. I'll continue with a rota, then. We finished talking to everyone who was reportedly here on Sunday morning. I don't think we learned much but some of it confirms things we'd been told." The constable handed over a sheaf of papers. "These are copies. I'll get it all recorded, of course."

"Good job, Thomas. Thank you. Reckon it's time to pack up here for today. Not that I'll switch off. You can't in these cases. It's with you twenty-four hours. A nasty business."

"Yes, Sir."

"Have you finished your shift?"

"I wish. I've been recalled to the station. Sergeant Barnes wants me to assist with a burglary. One of the seconded officers, DC Harper, is up at the crime scene twiddling his thumbs."

"Can I drop you off?"

"Thanks, Sir, but I fancy a walk. The weather's keeping up, nicely."

CHAPTER 5

Raymond Yates entered his Petworth apartment, dropped his briefcase beside the table in the lounge and pondered what to have for his evening meal.

Not for the first time he wished he had a Mary waiting for him, the dinner ready to be dished up. Marriage, he reckoned had to be a mixed blessing. The responsibilities and limitations of family life lined up against his present single status were often in his thoughts. At thirty-nine he had achieved a lot in the force but privately he guessed he'd never met the right woman. There had been numerous girlfriends but no lasting relationship, unless you counted Karen.

He'd gone out on and off for sometime with Karen and admitted he was fond of her. She was a lovely person and, come to think of it, a competent cook, and more importantly not attached to the police. Marriages between officers, he'd noted, rarely seemed to work. Most blamed the awkward hours they'd to cover. He liked Karen very much but was it enough to try to take their friendship to another level. He wasn't sure but he did sometimes envy guys like Harry who seemed to manage to maintain a blissful life whilst still operating as a police officer.

Yates went into his kitchen and took out a ready made

packet of spaghetti bolognaise from the freezer. Microwaved it would be ready in minutes. He switched on the television to hear the news. The local channel had caught up with the murder on the golf course, as they called it, and showed a picture of Fisborough and Carlton Greenhalgh. The report was brief, but it featured James Winter, Bradley Brown and Dougie Watson, all of whom spoke confidently. Bradley Brown, in particular, had regained his composure and seemed able to tell his story. Yates was frequently surprised how people responded to a starring role, guilty or otherwise. Investigators, he conceded, could learn a lot from media coverage, much as he hated it.

He listened to the rest of the news and accepted that a murder case always took over the whole of his life and everything else back-seated. Having eaten the bolognaise with no real relish, he resumed his perusal of the evidence so far. He concluded he had a long way to go before the case would open up and offer solutions. It was always a painstaking business.

The phone rang and he was drawn into a conversation with his mother about what to do for his 40th birthday next month.

"We have to hold a party, Darling. Everyone does these days, so make sure you're free. I thought we should book that new Italian restaurant in Park Grove. Phoebe was there last week and said the food was wonderful and they have a small dance floor. What do you think?"

"I think it's unnecessary."

"Don't be a spoil sport. It will take your mind off that ghastly job of yours."

Raymond Yates sighed his consent. Mother could go ahead and book on his sister's recommendation. Phoebe was usually reliable in her judgement. His mind had been diverted from the Greenhalgh case and he decided to go to bed and read something relaxing. Firstly, he'd have to phone Harry as promised.

"I'll meet you in the morning at the station and we'll take it from there. Any news?"

"Sorry, Chief, I got dragged into a burglary. Neighbours of mine, so I had to show an interest initially. I'm handing it on to the boys, though. They'll cope."

"Good show. Our murder needs your full attention. I'll up date you tomorrow."

Bed proved as relaxing as Ian Rankin allowed. It was possibly not the best material to read.

***

The good weather of the past few days developed over-night into cloud, wind and intermittent showers. The Detective Chief Inspector arrived at the station around 8.30am. Harry Barnes was in the entrance shaking an umbrella.

"Car's in for its MOT," he explained. "It had to be raining."

"Always the way," Yates agreed, "Can we find a place to ourselves?"

"My room okay? I'll let the others know not to disturb us."

"Fine."

Harry's room was little bigger than a traditional broom cupboard, but it housed the requisite chairs and a desk, which boasted an almost brand new computer and printer/duplicator and afforded as much privacy as could be expected in a small station.

"I approached Watson about the letter we found at Montgomery Square. The one he'd written to Carlton Greenhalgh."

"And?"

"He refused to give a satisfactory explanation. Said it was personal."

"I bet it was."

"Well, he knows we've seen that letter. We'll let him stew for a couple of days then find out if he's prepared to tell the story behind it. So, what do you think we should investigate today?"

"I supposed you'd tell me."

"There are a few loose ends to be tied up. Marian Chapman for instance. She indicated she'd seen Elizabeth Greenhalgh at the club early on Sunday morning. Elizabeth denies being there. I'll have to find out how certain the Chapman woman is. We'll try to establish if anyone else saw her, but that might be difficult. I have a feeling Babs Slater may hold the key to this case. I wonder if that Aunt of hers is still alive. If we trace her we could send someone to question her on what happened twenty-five or so years ago. About Babs and her baby and it could be worth inquiring into the baby's adoption?"

"So where do we begin?"

DCI Yates considered his Sergeant's question for a few seconds before deciding. "The rain's off. Let's take a stroll down to the club and see who's around firstly. It would be good to have a chat with Carlton Greenhalgh's golfing partners. Their statements didn't tell us much on Sunday and we have the mystery of the photo we found of Grant in Elizabeth Greenhalgh's bedroom drawer. It has to mean something. And those two women Chapman and Hawksworth. As I said before, we need to clear a few things up with the former anyway. Then we'll pay Babs Slater a visit. Let's hope she's more forthcoming than Watson. There's always the chance Carlton told her about Dougie's letter. Miracles do happen."

It was a fifteen minute brisk walk from the police station to the golf club. A watery sun had replaced the earlier showers so there was a possibility some stalwarts would be on the course.

"You know what they say. It never rains on a golf course. But I bet some of the members don't agree," Harry Barnes said.

"With the right gear a bit of summer rain can be refreshing. I once played in a storm over at Melford Grange. I was a guest and my partner assured me the weather would be fine despite it being dead close, and it was until the black clouds brought thunder, followed by lightening. We were as far out as we could be and the only shelter was your brolly and the trees and you're warned not to stand under the latter when there's lightening. I remember I was about to play a seven iron shot when there was a loud clap and a huge flash. I turned round to find my partner had dived into the nearest bunker, leaving me standing there petrified with my seven iron in my hand. Fortunately, it was my lucky day but I reckon that bolt struck within metres. I got the fright of my life and we got off those fairways and into the clubhouse as quickly as we could. I spent a good five minutes helping my friend brush sand out of his hair and off his clothes. It was one of the scariest moments I've ever experienced."

"You're right, Chief," Harry said, "You're very exposed out there. Several top golfers have had narrow escapes. I read somewhere that Lee Trevino has been struck at least twice and lived to tell the tale. All the main competition courses sound a Siren if lightening threatens but you don't get that warning on an ordinary course. You just have to use your common sense and come in at the first hint."

"Trouble is you can be so engrossed in your game you don't see it creeping up on you. At least today's not stormy."

The officers made their way into the clubhouse via the main entrance and encountered Agnes almost immediately.

"Can we have a couple of coffees please? One black one white and two sugars in each. Let's take a seat in the main lounge for a change. It looks pretty quiet."

They walked towards a table facing the full length windows. From there they could watch players drive from the first tee but they were more interested to see who was inside the clubhouse. A quick glance showed that Carlton's golfing partners weren't present, but Yates' ears pricked up when he recognised the distinctive voice of Marion Chapman before she even reached the dining lounge door.

"We're in luck," Yates said, nudging his sergeant. "The ladies have arrived."

The Detective Chief stood and beckoned Marion Chapman and Philippa Hawksworth to join them and the two women looked flustered but flattered to be invited. Agnes came through with the detectives' coffees and Yates ordered a further two cups for the lady members.

"How can we help you?" Marion asked once they were comfortably seated.

"I hope we're not interfering with any arrangements you have," the DCI began.

"Not at all," Philippa said. "We aren't playing today. Just dropped in for a coffee."

"That's good." DCI Yates turned to Marion. "I was hoping you'd confirm something for me. I believe you said you had seen Elizabeth Greenhalgh at the club on Sunday morning?"

"That's right. I was about to cross the front forecourt en route to the ladies' locker room when I saw her car pull up beside the trees just short of the clubhouse."

"Was anyone with her?"

"Not that I noticed, but the car was kind of secluded by the trees."

"What time was this exactly?"

"I can't be exact but I'd estimate it was quarter past nine. I recall thinking it was an unusual place to stop. Not many people frequent that area but there is a back path leading from it towards the professional shop. You could call it a short cut, I suppose, but it's not popularly used. The ground's too rough. And, you see, it's actually quicker to go through the clubhouse to the patio."

"You are absolutely certain it was Elizabeth you saw?"

"Well, yes. I'm convinced it was her car. It's such a distinctive shade of blue."

"Did you see Mrs Greenhalgh, herself?"

"I suppose not. But someone had to be driving the car, didn't they?"

"So if Elizabeth Greenhalgh says she wasn't anywhere near Fisborough that morning, she could be telling the truth?"

"I'd have sworn on oath it was her car. It's a BMW and I've never seen another, certainly not around here, in that colour. But if she says it wasn't her, I have to believe her."

DCI Yates nodded, but he wasn't so convinced about her last comment. His policy was to believe nothing until it was proved to be true.

"I assume you didn't see Mrs Greenhalgh or her car?" he said turning his attention to Philippa Hawksworth.

"Me? No. I was here before Marion and Elizabeth wasn't around then as far as I'm aware."

"Thank you, ladies. Now let's enjoy our coffees. Have you played golf for a long time?"

The conversation took on a general aspect as they

discussed the merits of the game of golf. As the officers rose to leave some minutes later, Sheenagh Davis came over to speak to them.

"I don't know if it's of any interest, Mr Yates, I've been keeping my ears open. I overheard a group of men talking about the murder earlier this morning. They were discussing the television news programme that featured Jack Winter with Dougie and Bradley. It was on last night."

"Yes," I saw it."

"They were saying something about Bradley being a cocky bastard. That was their language not mine, of course. And they said he had the hots for Babs big time and that they heard him threaten to have it out with Carlton a few days before he was killed." Sheenagh paused to see if the detective reacted, but Yates's expression remained impassive. "Well that's what they were saying. But loads of people say things like that without meaning it, don't they?"

"They do, indeed, Sheenagh, but…"

"Agnes also overheard Grant Mason saying it was ironic that Nick Baker declared he could kill Carlton for being late on Sunday morning. Grant, himself, isn't above suspicion. There's a rumour been circulating recently that he's been seeing quite a lot of Elizabeth Greenhalgh lately. Not that I've noticed. If it's true they are discreet not like Carlton and Babs. I tell you, my Jack says this club is a hive of infidelity. But, then, we're not paid to gossip. It's this murder, it gets your imagination working over- time, doesn't it?"

"Thank you, Sheenagh. Any information that might relate to the case is welcome, so keep listening."

Sheenagh went back to the kitchen with a smug smile and DCI Yates was grinning as he left with Harry Barnes.

"Seems we've got a few unpaid undercover cops on the

premises, Harry."

"Let's hope they can give us a useful lead," Sergeant Barnes replied. "So where now?"

"Back to your cosy little office. We'll do the usual run through and list the order of follow ups. We have to go over and over everything stacks of times in case we've missed something. And, yes it can be tiring, but it is necessary routine procedure. We'll draw up a plan for tomorrow. It's going to include yet another visit to Montgomery Square and a further chat with Dougie Watson. I'm deliberately leaving that young man to his thoughts in the hope he'll open up, but don't count on it."

They began the walk back to the Police Station and were glad they'd brought their umbrellas as the rain returned in earnest.

"Getting anywhere with your neighbour's burglary?" Yates asked

"Haven't had much time to catch up with it. Maybe I could grab a few minutes this afternoon to check."

"Do what you have to. Can't be easy for you keeping up with both jobs. Are you still glad you opted to join the murder investigating team?"

"Definitely."

"Good. I'm hoping they've come up with some DNA evidence to make our job easier. It might take a bit longer to get results."

Back at the station there was nothing from the DNA boys. DCI Yates reckoned a call wasn't out of order.

"Hi, DCI Yates, here. I was wondering if you had anything on the Greenhalgh murder?"... Is that all, then.... Okay let us have it as soon as possible.... Thanks very much."

Harry Barnes looked at his Chief quizzically as the latter

replaced the phone.

DCI Yates shrugged. "They're still analysing his clothes etc. The golf club provided precisely nothing, as I expected. We should begin collecting samples from known contacts for comparison with any evidence they do manage to come up with. We'll add that to tomorrow's schedule."

"I've been reading through the statements we gathered on Sunday again. Haven't come up with anything new yet." Barnes said.

"Okay, two heads are better than one. So we'll go through them together. Let's start with Mason and Baker."

"Sounds like a firm of accountants or lawyers" the sergeant quipped.

"That's not so funny as it sounds. If memory serves me right, Baker is a CA and Mason is a legal secretary."

"There you go," Harry laughed. "Their jobs must have lodged in my sub-conscience. I've fixed to check up on my burglary at four. Hope that's okay?"

"That gives us forty-five minutes then. Do you realise we skipped lunch today? I'll order a sandwich and coffee to be sent in."

The two officers swapped opinions as they read through Sunday's statements. WPC Pauline Fergus came in with a tray containing the drinks and some ham and cheese sandwiches, placed it on the sergeant's desk and left.

"Attractive young constable that." Yates remarked as his eyes followed her out of the room.

"Yes, she's showing a lot of potential. Unfortunately she's not available on the social front. She's got a boyfriend and he's a big lad whose interests are rugby and boxing."

"Thanks for the info'. I'll make sure I behave."

The pile of statements was reduced by half by the time Harry Barnes left to meet his team. DCI Yates pushed the remainder aside and scribbled a note to Harry and went home. It was only half past four but Raymond Yates knew from past experience when to take a break. A murder inquiry was an intense business and batteries had to be recharged from time to time. He admitted to feeling tired and decided he'd sit back, catch up with a bit of television and then nip down to his local for a meal and a pint before settling for a comparatively early night. That way he'd be refreshed to tackle the heavy schedule he'd set up for the next day. He hoped Harry Barnes would follow suit but guessed he'd try to spend some time with Mary.

CHAPTER 6

The early night resulted in an early morning for DCI Yates. When he arrived at the Police Station, the cleaners were just knocking off. It was six-thirty and he was eager to get on. He took out the sheaf of statements and decided to carry on looking at them himself. It was boring but necessary.

Harry Barnes joined him around half eight.

"Any luck?" he asked, indicating the documents.

"Not really. A few confirmations and a little more insight into Greenhalgh's character. Did you know he fancied himself as a singer and was a keen poker player, who wasn't averse to having a gamble? He doesn't seem to have got in deep with the gambling, though. No debts or disputes in that field, so it's not likely to feature in his murder. I still have a strong feeling the solution to this case will lie close to home and Fisborough Golf Club.

"That's been my view from the start. There are many diverse characters among the golfers. The key has to be at the club or within his family. Who'd have thought a simple game could lead to such complicated relationships?"

"There's nothing simple about the game of golf, Harry. But it's people who are complicated. The lives they lead, the relationships they form, the way they see themselves and their position in the world they've built up over the years.

At fifty-eight, Carlton Greenhalgh probably considered life was rapidly moving on. Maybe he felt unsure of his marriage, of his standing at Fisborough, and with retirement looming, his work even. My guess is he was a proud guy who sought the respect of others but was in danger of losing it."

"I see where you're coming from. His affair with Babs Slater didn't do a lot to enhance his reputation at Fisborough but there are some would say good luck to him. His wife appears to be a cold fish. He's not the first to have strayed from such a marriage."

"Maybe being single has its compensations. But enough of this philosophising. Let's get down to work. I drew up a rough schedule for today. I considered bringing in Elizabeth Greenhalgh for further questioning but this office is a bit cramped, so how about we start by going to Montgomery Square and quizzing Elizabeth about Carlton's will and that photograph of Grant Mason. See if the wife, herself, was doing a bit of philandering."

The route to Montgomery Square was becoming a familiar one. Harry felt a tinge of envy as they approached the large houses. Mary would love to live here but this area was out with his means now and in the future, unless he won the lottery.

The door of number 19 was opened by Elizabeth. She was casually dressed in a navy sweater and slacks and her hair hung loosely about her shoulders making her seem more approachable and in a way more attractive.

She ushered them in saying, "Well at least ten o'clock is a reasonable time to call. Thank you for that. I do have to go out in forty minutes, however. I wish you'd give prior notice."

"The surprise element goes with the job. Catching

people unawares often brings results. I do appreciate it might not be so convenient for you and we do risk you being out, but this time you're not and we're here. We need to clear a few things up."

Elizabeth Greenhalgh smiled, enhancing her appearance still further.

"I realise you have a job to do and like it or not I have to be involved. Can I offer you tea or coffee?"

"No thanks, this is purely a working visit."

Harry looked slightly disappointed. He was never one to reject a cuppa.

DCI Yates and Sergeant Barnes accepted a seat in the elegantly furnished lounge and the former continued his inquiries.

"I hope you found everything was left to your satisfaction after our last visit?"

"Apart from a few creases in my duvet cover, yes. I'm surprised you even found it necessary to search my room."

"Where a serious crime has been committed, we leave no stone unturned. It was within the rights of our warrant to include your room and as it happens I do have to question you on something we found there. I had intended to bring it up as a secondary issue but as you have mentioned your room I have to point out a photograph of Grant Mason was discovered in your bedside drawer. It struck us as odd. Maybe you can offer us an explanation?"

Elizabeth's relaxed manner stiffened. "I could, but is it relevant to your inquiries?"

"That we don't know but it could be. We could draw our own conclusions and they might not be accurate."

There was a long pause before Elizabeth Greenhalgh spoke.

"Chief Inspector..." she began.

"Detective Chief Inspector," he interrupted.

"Detective Chief Inspector, I have nothing to hide. Surely my private life deserves to remain private?"

"Of course, you have our word it will not become public unless it has a bearing on your husband's murder."

"Grant Mason and I are very good friends. We share a passion for classical music and opera in particular, and, yes, we have gone to concerts and dinner together. But I hope I don't disappoint you when I say we are not lovers, though I admit to being very fond of Grant. He was a friend to Carlton as well and as you probably know they were golfing partners of many years standing. Recently we considered taking our friendship to a different level but we are both married although Grant has been separated from his wife for several years."

DCI Yates said, "Your son Edward indicated to us that you were contemplating divorce. He didn't suggest Grant Mason was behind that move."

"I should think not. As far as I'm aware, my son has no idea of my feelings towards Grant. He does know we've been to the concert hall together."

"Thank you for being honest with us. We get no pleasure out of asking delicate questions. And now I have to ask another. When we came here the other day you and Edward indicated you were going to see your solicitor. As no copy of a will was found among Carlton's effects, we wondered if you had taken it with you?"

"I'll grant you don't miss much. Yes, we took the will into Geoffrey Hamilton, our lawyer. It may have seemed a little quick but I knew he was going away within the next few days and wanted to set the ball rolling, as they say. Apart from a few minor amounts to charity and a somewhat ridiculous bequest to Babs Slater, the main part of the estate is divided between me and Edward. Does that satisfy you?"

"Thank you again. Please give Sergeant Barnes Mr Hamilton's details. We will need to verify what you have told us."

"Of course," Elizabeth jotted down the requested details and handed them to Harry Barnes. "Now if you'll excuse me I have to get ready to go out."

"Before we leave, can you tell us if your husband had any dealings with the Fisborough Golf Club Professional?"

"Not to my knowledge, except for the odd purchase from his shop. Mr Watson's only been at the club a few months."

***

"As interviews go," Harry Barnes said, as they headed back to the station, "that wasn't too hurtful."

"No. Our Elizabeth seemed to thaw a bit along with her flowing locks. She even offered us tea."

"Did you believe what she told us about her and Grant Mason?"

"I'm inclined to. Never close my mind, however. The information about the will was interesting. I'd like to know how much Babs Slater has been left. I bet that didn't please his wife and it doesn't imply he regarded Babs as, what was it? A something nuisance."

"Want me to contact Hamilton when we get back?"

"Yes, see if he can fit us in before he goes away."

"Will do."

DCI Yates picked up the day's schedule and deleted Montgomery Square. Next on his list was Dougie Watson.

Harry Barnes put down the telephone, "I've fixed up Geoffrey Hamilton for nine in the morning. I suggested we went to his offices but he said he was due to visit a client in the vicinity of this station and said he'd drop in here first. I explained what it was about and he promised to come armed with a copy of the will. Tomorrow night he's on his way to Tenerife for a week, lucky devil."

"Are you and Mary going away this year?"

"Depends if we decide to afford a holiday. We might take the odd weekend instead."

"Solve this case with me and I'll put you down for a bonus."

"Now, that would be welcome. We could do with a break." Harry beamed at his superior.

"Detective Superintendent Carter comes back from his trip to the Great Wall of China tonight. He'll be looking for a report on this case tomorrow. I'll pad out where we've got to so far but I'd like to have more to tell him. I'm going to the golf course after lunch. Hope to shake up young Dougie. Any chance you can join me?"

"It should be okay. The guys here are coping fine. Makes me feel I'm redundant."

"You're proving very useful to me, Harry. We seem to click as a team. I'm enjoying having you on board. Makes a change to some of the chaps I've worked with."

"Thanks, Sir, I'm flattered."

"Let's see if someone can knock up some sandwiches and a coffee and we'll be off to the Golf Club. Can't afford to let hem forget what we look like."

***

Harry Barnes was behind the wheel as they drove in silence to Fisborough Golf Club.

On arrival they headed straight to the Professional Shop. Pushing the door open, they bumped into Babs Slater as she was leaving.

DCI Yates paused to speak to her.

"How are you coping?"

"I was feeling a little better today, so decided to come to

the club for the first time since Sunday. It's not been easy."

The detective smiled sympathetically. "I doubt if it has. I'm afraid we'll need to speak to you again soon and you'll be contacted about giving a DNA sample. It's a routine process and only takes a minute or two. Everyone who had contact with Carlton will be approached in the next few days. You will be aware that DNA is a valuable tool in establishing both guilt and innocence. It has to be backed up with other hard evidence, however, hence the need for questioning."

Babs nodded to show she understood and went on her way. Yates turned to Dougie Watson who was unpacking a delivery of balls and gloves.

"Are you alone, Dougie?"

"Looks like it doesn't it?" The professional's reply was cool. "I'm very busy."

"Okay. We'll keep it short. Have you anything else you'd like to tell us?"

"No."

"You mentioned having invoices regarding the money you asked Mr Greenhalgh to give you. Any chance we could see them?"

"Not right now. I've still to look them out."

"You've had a couple of days to do that already. I'm going to request you bring the information into our offices sometime tomorrow. One other thing. I don't suppose you saw Mrs Greenhalgh at the club early Sunday morning?"

"I don't recall seeing her."

"Right, that's all for now but remember to drop in tomorrow. I don't know if you heard my conversation with Ms Slater, but you will be asked to supply a DNA sample as routine. Perhaps you could do that at the same time?"

DougieWatson made no response as he turned his back

on the police officers and continued to unpack and display his delivery. Yates and Barnes left him to it.

"Not very communicative, that lad." Harry Barnes observed.

"No. But looking into his eyes, I felt his defiance was weakening a little. I think he'll crack before long."

They went through the patio doors into the dining lounge. Agnes was rearranging the tables.

"We've a quiz organised for tonight. It's our first function since …."

"Glad things are getting back to normal," the DCI interrupted. "Do you think we could have a word with Sheenagh?"

"I expect so. We're not busy yet. Not 'til lunch time anyway."

She disappeared into the kitchen and emerged again with the steward's wife.

"You wanted me?" Sheenagh asked, wiping her hands on her apron.

"I wondered if you had seen Mrs Greenhalgh here at the club early on Sunday morning? Marion Chapman believes she saw her car."

"She's pretty sharp, is Marion. Not one to make mistakes but no, I can't say I personally saw Elizabeth. I'll ask around if you like. Discreetly, of course. If that BMW of hers was here you could hardly miss it. It's one of a kind."

"Thanks, Sheenagh. That will be very helpful."

The two officers walked out towards their car.

"What it is to have an extra pair of ears and eyes on the job, Harry," Yates said, not for the first time.

"If anyone can come up with something that woman will. Look whose coming? Hi, Greg. Anything to report?"

"Nothing useful, Sir. I've just been up to the van. The

constable manning it is fed up. Says there's been no activity since yesterday lunchtime. He feels he's wasting his time and could be more useful down at the station.

DCI Yates hesitated for a moment as he contemplated what PC Thomas was saying. "I reckon he's right. I'll arrange for the van to be taken off the site in the morning. Will you let the team know."

"Yes, Sir. Right now, Sir."

Yates and Barnes drove away as Greg retraced his steps to the murder site.

"Satisfied that's the right move. I thought you wanted a presence on the course."

"No-one seems to have anything to say to our guys out there and we are short of manpower. It's time to assess where we are and decide on our next move. I'm really keen to get hold of DNA samples from all who may have had contact with the victim. Draw up a list and we'll notify them this afternoon and call them in for tomorrow. The sooner the samples reach the lab' the sooner comparisons can be made when they've finished with Greenhalgh and his gear. Let's hope something shows up. We need a break. I was considering going to see Babs Slater but I think I'll try to catch her at the station if she puts in an appearance."

"Sounds a good idea." Harry tried to sound enthusiastic. They did seem to be dragging their heels.

"So let's start again where we left off with those statements and pray for some insight. I vote we treat ourselves to a bar meal before getting back to the grindstone."

With their stomachs satisfied, the DCI and his Sergeant got down to the painstaking study and spent the next two hours sifting through the little evidence they had accrued.

"You know, Chief, I can't help thinking Marion

Chapman was right about seeing Elizabeth Greenhalgh. Call it intuition or whatever."

"Assuming that to be the case, what brought her to the Golf Club on Sunday? I wonder why she wasn't playing in the Laureston Open with the other ladies. Babs Slater said most of the good players were there and I checked the locker room lists. Elizabeth plays off fourteen and in terms of the ladies' game that indicates she's a useful player."

"Maybe, like Babs, she didn't get a time."

"You could be right, but I'd have thought Mrs Greenhalgh had a few strings to pull and she is the lady vice-captain. But perhaps we're clutching at straws. Why does she need a special reason to come to her own club? The thing is she denies being there and until we prove otherwise we have to give her the benefit of the doubt."

"She might have been trying to see Grant Mason before his game with Nick and Carlton was due to tee off. Someone other than Marion could have spotted her. We'll just have to wait and see if Sheenagh finds anything out."

They didn't have much longer to wait. As the detectives were preparing to call it a day, the phone in Harry's office rang. It seemed Sheenagh Davis had mentioned her mission to her husband, who was able to confirm that he had noticed the BMW parked under the trees as he came back from walking their dog, Rufus. There was no sign of Elizabeth but he had no doubt it was her car."

"So she wasn't telling us the truth, which suggests she's concealing something. The question is what and is it relevant to our inquiry?

"I wonder why Davis didn't mention taking the dog for a walk that morning. He gave the impression he hadn't left the clubhouse."

CHAPTER 7

The Police Station was rocking the next morning. Sergeant Harry Barnes had been in touch with all those who might have been in contact with Carlton Greenhalgh on the morning of his murder and invited them to call in at the police station between ten and twelve. A steady flow of possible suspects had responded. It would be interesting Harry thought to see who didn't turn up.

Yates was conferring with Detective Superintendent Carter at the district headquarters and was expected to be away until the afternoon. Harry took the opportunity to catch up with the outcome of the recent burglary. He was happy to learn that an arrest had been made and some of the stolen goods returned to his neighbour. The culprits were a couple of youngsters from the Foxhill Estate, an area noted for breeding criminal offenders. The lads concerned had been in trouble before and would be facing a custodial sentence. In an odd way, Harry Barnes felt pity for them. They hadn't got a chance. Their fathers had spent most of their days in prison and their mothers hadn't the ability to cope. Anyone coming out of the Foxhill Estate had a doubtful future and more needed to be done to educate them and help them understand there were other ways of earning a living than thieving. They'd had some success with setting up a football team but it was difficult to get other teams to agree to give them a match. The Foxhill name meant trouble and people in the villages around Fisborough were law abiding citizens. Except it seemed when it came to murder.

Harry was enjoying working with DCI Yates. He was a decent cop who rarely pulled rank and appreciated those who made an effort. He liked the way Yates didn't jump to conclusions and kept an open mind. He'd watched and listened carefully during the interviews the DCI had conducted and was impressed by the way he handled people.

Harry knew Elizabeth Greenhalgh was lined up for another grilling. That morning he'd gone down to the Golf Club to check what Jack Davis had told his wife. The steward hadn't much to say but he confirmed he'd seen Elizabeth's car at the spot indicated by the Chapman woman. There was, he said, another car parked a little further up the road, however, he wasn't sure of its make, but it was possibly a Honda. It was silver, a colour common to a lot of cars belonging to club members.

He was sorry he'd omitted to tell them he'd walked the dog that morning. Dogs weren't allowed on the course so he routinely took the path up to the high field and the fairways couldn't be seen along the route because of the trees. His walk usually lasted fifteen minutes and he estimated he'd noted the car sometime before eight-thirty but he couldn't be sure, because he wasn't keeping tabs on the clock. He had thought it an odd place for Elizabeth Greenhalgh to park but he'd seen it there on a couple of occasions and he hadn't realised the police would be interested in it.

Harry had taken notes and prepared a detailed report for Yates when he came in. At lunch time he enjoyed a tuna sandwich meal packed by Mary and complemented it with canteen tea. The canteen at Fisborough Police Station hardly merited the name. It was a shed-like building with a corrugated iron roof sited in the grounds behind the offices. There was enough room for three tables and a dozen plastic seats, no oven, but a hob and grill on which they could boil an egg and fry a rasher of bacon. At one time they'd had Freda, a woman who catered for them, but she wasn't replaced when she left to have a baby and everyone fended for themselves. Everyone that is except the DCI and senior visiting officers who called on an available constable to rustle up teas and coffees. It was typical of most country police stations and it suited Harry. Up to now he'd never wanted to work anywhere else and probably never would, but he liked the challenge presented by the Greenhalgh case.

As expected the DCI was back at Fisborough Police Station by three-fifteen in the afternoon. The meeting with Detective Superintendent Carter had gone well enough and the latter had appeared reasonably satisfied with the report he'd been handed. He stressed the need to move the case forward; to strike while the iron was still hot. Seeing it was a five iron that had killed Carlton Greenhalgh it was an apt expression.

Babs Slater walked into the Station as arranged at half past three. She looked a dejected figure, as if tired through lack of sleep. Her hair appeared to have lost its curly bounce along with her step. The DCI was in the reception area when she entered. WPC Pauline Fergus was in charge of taking the DNA swabs and Yates suggested this should take place first and once completed, he requested Babs Slater should be shown into the office he was sharing with Sergeant Barnes.

Babs Slater made no objections. DCI Yates went along the corridor to join Harry in the compact space in which they worked together.

He was greeted with a cheery, "Good afternoon, Sir." Even yet, Harry still sometimes forgot to drop the formalities.

"Good afternoon, Sergeant," the DCI replied, pointedly, a grin lightening his face. Harry grinned back, "Old habits die hard, Sir," and they both laughed.

Their attitude changed when Babs was brought through to one in keeping with investigating officers.

"Thank you for agreeing to speak to us, Ms Slater. "Do you have anything you wish to add to your previous statements that might help us with our inquiries?"

"I don't think so."

"When we bumped into you yesterday, you were coming out of the Fisborough professional's shop, but I observed you weren't carrying anything to suggest you'd made a purchase. What was the purpose of your visit?"

Babs looked uncomfortable. She paused before answering.

"Nothing really. I quite often drop in on Dougie to browse round the latest clothing and equipment. I was considering a new sweater but nothing appealed to me."

"I see. Are you aware Mr Greenhalgh has included you in his will?"

A faint blush spread across Babs Slater's pale cheeks. "I'd no idea. Has he?"

"According to his wife, yes. His solicitor wasn't in touch with you before he went on holiday to Tenerife?"

"No."

"I guess he didn't have the time. So you are unable to tell us the amount involved?"

"Of course, not. This has taken me by surprise," Babs looked flustered. Suddenly, her expression changed. "I hope you don't see this as a motive for killing Carlton. That would be absurd. I find it difficult to kill a wasp and I can't stand them. I was very close to Carlton. I would never hurt him."

"But you were seen arguing with him shortly before his death. According to our witness you were, to quote, 'pushing him about'."

"But I've already explained that."

"Yes, I know. You'd be amazed how many people change what they've previously told us. Are you quite sure you have nothing else to add?"

"Positive. Can I go now?"

"Yes, though as always we may need to speak to you again."

Babs Slater left the office, a troubled expression aging her face.

"Hope I wasn't too tough with her. But I have a feeling that woman could tell us a lot more. She's keeping something back, Harry, and I'd love to know what."

Harry nodded in agreement. Whatever it was, Babs Slater was not prepared to tell them yet. Within seconds Elizabeth Greenhalgh was ushered into the room. In contrast to Babs, she portrayed an air of confidence.

"Good afternoon, Officers. I believe you wish to see me. Having been made to give a DNA sample by that young WPC, I was then faced with Babs Slater. She looked awful. Whatever you said to her appears to have caused her some distress. She was crying and I almost felt sorry for her. I sincerely hope you don't reduce me to tears."

"That depends on how you react to our questioning, Mrs Greenhalgh."

"Well, let's get this over with. I'm a busy lady."

DCI Yates got down to business. "There are two things we absolutely hate. The first is people who waste our time and the second is people who fail to tell us the truth. You fall into the second category."

"And what makes you come to that conclusion?"

"We asked you if you were in the vicinity of Fisborough Golf Club early on the morning of your husband's murder. You implied you'd been nowhere near the club. We now have two reliable sightings of your BMW parked just short of the course. We have seen the car in your drive. It is a very distinctive colour and it would be surprising if our witnesses are both mistaken. So I ask you again. Were you anywhere near the course at around eight-thirty on the morning your husband was killed?"

Elizabeth Greenhalgh looked steadily at the DCI as she replied. "It would not, I presume, be in my interests to deny it. But I do object to what I consider to be an intrusion into my privacy."

"Object away. We are dealing with a very violent death and whilst we may hate having to probe into your personal life as much as you do, it is part of our job. We have to unearth all the evidence we can and weigh it up if our investigations are to be brought to a satisfactory conclusion. Concealing evidence is an offence and doesn't help us. We need you to be completely honest. Please, tell us the purpose behind your visit that morning?"

Elizabeth Greenhalgh kept her composure as she considered her answer. "As it seems I'm not allowed a private life, I guess I have to 'come clean'. I believe that's the expression used. Just after my husband left for the golf course, I received a call from Grant Mason. He needed to speak to me urgently and we arranged to meet outside the Fisborough Course."

"We've been given to understand you have met there on previous occasions."

"That's true. I parked my car under the trees and walked back up the hill a little. When Grant pulled up beside me, I got in his car to hear what he wanted to tell me." Elizabeth stopped at this point but was prompted to continue.

"We need to know the gist of your conversation."

"You already know Grant and I are friends. He had been pressing me lately to leave Carlton and make our own relationship more permanent. I'm sure I admitted that before. He told me he had received a letter offering him a post in America. He wanted me to be the first to know and hoped I'd join him there. Now, you know."

"Well, thank you for explaining to us. What did you say to him? Were you prepared to leave your husband?"

"I told him it wasn't that easy and I'd need time to think it over. Are you married Detective Chief Inspector?"

"No, but Sergeant Barnes is."

"He'll understand, then. I'd been married to Carlton for a good many years. We had a comfortable lifestyle, a lovely home that I helped to set up and am very attached to. It is true ours was an odd relationship and physically not ideal. Over the years I'd got used to my husband's indiscretions, his wayward ways. I didn't like it very much but I wasn't sure if I wanted to give up on my marriage completely. If I were a widow or divorced it would be different but I was still married to Carlton and, believe it or not, that meant something. All those years aren't easily dismissed."

"And when you explained how you felt to Grant Mason, how did he take it?"

"Grant is a very sensible, down to earth type of man. He said he could wait for my decision and admitted my marriage to Carlton was a problem but he was sure we could overcome it. He pointed out how much he liked being with me, how much I meant to him and emphasised the things we had in common. He was quite persuasive."

"So Grant Mason saw Carlton as an obstacle in any future you might have together?"

Elizabeth Greenhalgh looked startled. "I did not mean to imply Grant had a motive for getting rid of Carlton. You have to know the man to accept that he was too rational a being to ever contemplate killing someone. He might have wanted to be with me but Carlton was still his friend. They had been golfing partners for a long time."

"But that friendship hadn't prevented him becoming close to you."

Elizabeth got up from her chair. "The idea of Grant being in any way concerned with Carlton's killing is preposterous. If you don't mind, I'd like to leave,"

The investigating officers let her go,

"Phew," Harry Barnes exclaimed. "She fairly rose to Grant Mason's defence."

"Possibly rightly so. He'd have to be a pretty cool customer to commit a murder and then within minutes wait on the tee for the guy he'd bumped off. But what we've just learned is interesting."

"So I guess you're keeping an open mind as always?"

"Exactly. I take it you managed to make some comprehensive notes, Harry?"

Harry nodded. "I'll type them up and let you have them. Am I glad I studied shorthand. Why don't you make these interviews more formal so that we can record them directly."

"I want to save folk the expense of feeling they need a solicitor. That will come once we have more concrete evidence. We're not even close to that stage. Has Grant Mason come in to give DNA, yet?"

"I've no idea but I'll find out."

Harry Barnes left the office to speak to Pauline Fergus

and learned Mason had been among the first to have a swab taken, along with Nick Baker and about a dozen others.

"Is it all right if I pack up, Sir?" she asked. "My shift should have finished about twenty minutes ago and my boyfriend's waiting."

"Of course. Thanks for staying on. I assume your work notes are up to date?"

Pauline confirmed they were and went off to meet her Rugby player.

Harry made his way back to his office to pass the news on to his chief.

"We'll speak to Mason again tomorrow. I'm going home now to spend the evening contemplating what Babs and Elizabeth have told us."

The wife and her would be lover and the victim's mistress, he thought – what an intriguing combination but were any of them likely to be involved in Carlton Greenhalgh's demise?"

CHAPTER 8

DCI Yates and Sergeant Harry Barnes pulled up outside the address given by Grant Mason in his original statement on the day Carlton Greenhalgh died. The block of flats was impressive but could never compete with Elizabeth's grand detached house. Yates could understand why she was reluctant to swap her current home to live here with Grant, four floors up, with a balcony but no garden, although it did boast a lift. America could present a different proposition.

Grant Mason was enjoying a breakfast of sardines on toast when the officers arrived.

"Come in. I do have to leave for work in fifteen minutes. Got to pay the mortgage."

"We'll do our best to accommodate your time schedule. Something has cropped up which we need to verify."

"Okay. I'll try to help."

"Yesterday we questioned Mrs Greenhalgh about the early morning visit she paid to Fisborough Golf Course on the day of her husband's murder. I suspect she will have contacted you concerning this. She told us you wanted to speak to her and arranged to meet her outside the club. We know you are quite close to Elizabeth. She led us to believe you wanted her to leave her husband to set up home with you. Is that right?"

"I was expecting you to call at some time. Yes, Carlton didn't deserve Elizabeth. He treated her very shabbily. We were very good friends at one time but over the years he changed. I guess I was sorry for his wife at first but we found we shared a love of classical music and our friendship grew from that. I don't think Carlton had a clue how we felt about each other. He was too wrapped up in his own little affairs to pay any attention to Elizabeth and her needs."

"I understand you are considering a position abroad and hoped Mrs Greenhalgh would join you. How did you feel when she said she needed time? That it wouldn't be easy to walk out on her marriage?"

"How do you think I felt? I wasn't exactly elated. I've to accept or reject the offer by the end of next week. It's a big opportunity but Elizabeth plays an important part in my life. I needed to establish where our relationship stood. I didn't want her to hear from any of my colleagues about the move, so it was urgent I got in touch with her."

"What did you do once you'd spoken to her?"

"I drove on into the car park, got out my gear and waited for Nick Baker to arrive. We went round to the first tee just before ten. I expected to see Carlton there because he was usually the first to arrive but he wasn't. In fact I was pleased I didn't have to face him having just tried to persuade Elizabeth to leave him. It wouldn't have been a comfortable round."

"And Elizabeth Greenhalgh? What did she do?"

"Went straight home, I believe."

"Were you angry?"

"Yes I was, but not enough to follow him and Babs Slater to the practice area."

"You saw them?"

"Yes, he was carrying a golf club and she had her bag.

Ostensibly going to practice."

"You didn't attempt to contact them?"

"No."

"Why didn't you tell Mr Baker you'd seen him?"

"I don't know. Perhaps it was because I was inwardly angry."

"And is that all you can tell us, Mr Mason?"

"Yes. And I really do have to go to work now."

DCI Yates and Sergeant Barnes followed Grant out of his flat and watched as he drove off in his silver Honda.

"Jack Davis's silver car. The one he saw parked up the road from Elizabeth's BMW," Harry Barnes observed.

"The very one, I guess, Harry."

Back at the Police Station, DCI Yates resumed the task of assessing evidence. Harry Barnes arranged to meet his team for a briefing. The recent burglary was solved but a road accident involving two cars and a lorry needed investigating and the mystery disappearance of a pedigree, prize winning dog would keep his men, and women, busy. He met up with Yates for lunch and the pair decided their local pub offered the best deal. The afternoon was spent on routine duties. Detective Superintendent Carter was looking for an update and Yates was happy to impart details of their progress. At least things were moving forward even though at a slow pace. The big breakthrough was yet to come. DCI Yates was confident it would.

The following morning both officers were engaged in analysing their findings so far. The list of suspects remained the same- in no particular order - Mrs Elizabeth Greenhalgh, her son Edward, who had been very low key up to now, Grant Mason, Babs Slater, Bradley Brown, who hadn't been seen for days and was due a call from the investigating officers because he had failed to turn up to provide the required DNA sample. Dougie Watson was also listed as a main suspect. Making up the list of extras were James Winter, Jack Davis, Callum Martin and another six hundred unnamed members of Fisborough Golf Club. The task of the investigating team was to eliminate all but one. Unless, of course, two or more people were responsible for Carlton Greenhalgh's death.

The DCI prepared to go home, having spent the rest of his day on routine work. He was frustrated that rather than becoming clearer the investigation was getting more complicated, but he knew this was often the case. Harry had been preoccupied with some minor local incidents for most of the day. Yates picked up his brief case and was about to leave the office when the phone rang.

"Hi Chief…Mike Chainey here – DNA…... Thought you might like this bit of news in advance of getting our full report tomorrow. I say full but Bradley Brown and a few others have still to be swabbed."

"We're aware of that Mike. I'm hoping to see him tomorrow and I'll make sure we collect a sample."

"Good, well I was about to tell you something very interesting that has cropped up. Not sure how relevant it is, but Babs Slater and Dougie Watson have matching DNA."

"They what?" Yates threw down his brief case and sat down. "There's no way you're mistaken? So that means…."

"They have to be related in some way. I'll email you the rest of the results in the morning. We're about to shut down for the night. It's been all go today."

Mike Chainey, head of the DNA Department, rang off.

Yates took a deep breath. Babs and Dougie… was it possible he was her son? The age difference was probably right and they were hardly likely to be cousins. It seemed incredible, yet credible at the same time. They had fair hair in common but nothing else. She was small, he was tall and well built. If they shared their DNA, at first glance, they didn't appear to share their looks. Was this the break they needed? It was certainly an interesting revelation and one they would need to follow up right away.

The DCI went off in search of Sergeant Barnes. He had no difficulty locating him in the reception area. Harry was lecturing one of his junior constables on a procedure of some kind, but he stopped when he saw Yates coming towards him.

"We need to talk, Sergeant."

Harry Barnes could tell from Yates' manner that it was something important. He dropped everything and followed his superior into their office room. Yates imparted the news he'd received from DNA.

"Do you conclude the same as me? Are the pair mother and son?" Yates asked.

"I suppose it's the likeliest conclusion. The ages are correct."

"That's what occurred to me, Harry." DCI Yates picked up his brief case again. "Look, I'm going home to think this through, then sleep on it. Tomorrow's going to be a busy day."

Harry whistled as he went into the duty room and put up a schedule for his lads to follow in the morning. The sergeant informed PC Thomas that he would be working solely on the Greenhalgh case the following day and asked Thomas to see that the other matters ran smoothly. Harry headed home to Mary and a steak pie dinner. Like Yates he had a lot to consider. He phoned the DCI to remind him they had an appointment with Bradley Brown at nine.

"Thanks for that, Harry. With what's turned up I had

forgotten. I suppose we'll have to see Brown as arranged first before we can tackle the other two. Who do you think we should speak to after him, Babs or Dougie?

"I'd suggest Babs. She's more forthcoming than her son, if that's who he is."

"Good point. Dougie will have to open once she spills the beans. There's no mention of a connection between Watson and Greenhalgh, unless that's in tomorrow's report. Maybe he's not the father. Which leaves Bradley Brown as the likely seducer as the findings rule out Carlton's brother Kevin, too. I understand he's coming back to the UK because of what's happened. I mean to speak to him but for obvious reasons he isn't top priority. I can't wait to get Brown's DNA test results. This could be a huge development in the case. Let's hope our luck's in. I'll see you around eight - eight thirty in the morning. Have an early night if you can."

"Not much chance of that. My in-laws are visiting. The women are off to the Bingo and I'll be entertaining Mary's dad to a few beers in the Barnes's lounge."

"Well, do your best. We'll both need to be in good form."

***

The investigating team were waiting in the interview room long before Bradley Brown was due to appear. They had agreed to say nothing about the shock news they'd received the day before to Bradley because at this stage it might not concern him as far as they knew. Unfortunately, Babs indicated she couldn't make it to the police station until eleven in the morning, so Dougie was asked to call in at ten-thirty and Babs half an hour later. It wasn't what they had wanted but as they would probably wish to speak to them together, they would ask the professional to wait until after Babs had been questioned. He might well refuse but they'd take a chance on that.

Bradley arrived on time. He apologised for not turning up the previous day, saying he had been feeling unwell and he provided the sample when requested with no objections. Yates understood the guy had a reputation as a joker but he was certainly keeping his talent hidden. The DCI guessed the fooling around was a cover for a lack of confidence. Several well-known comedians used their art to bluff their way through life. In other words they had duel personalities.

DCI Yates asked Bradley Brown to repeat how he had discovered Carlton Greenhalgh's body and his actions thereafter. To his credit the account tallied exactly with what he'd told them earlier.

"And you're quite certain you didn't see anyone else in the vicinity?"

"I got a fright when I came on the body and panicked a bit. I honestly wasn't aware of seeing anyone. All I wanted to do was get back to the clubhouse and warn the staff before other players found him. It wasn't a pretty sight and I thought the ladies in particular would be in hysterics if they came across him. There was a lot of blood. It turned my stomach and I haven't been near the course since. I just haven't felt up to it."

"But you were able to appear on television the following evening."

"They approached us to go to the studios. They were very persistent. I felt okay because I was with James Winter and Dougie and not on my own."

The DCI refrained from saying he had appeared more than just okay at being interviewed by the presenter. In fact he'd been the most talkative of the threesome. Yates needed to keep Bradley on their side for the questions he was about to ask.

"I understand you knew Babs Slater when she first lived in Fisborough as a young girl."

"I was brought up in the village and so was Babs. We went to school together, though she was always a year or two behind me. We were never classmates but we were always friendly. It's like that in a village community. Everyone knows everyone."

"Am I correct in saying you and Babs were more than just friends when you were in your teens?"

"There's no point in denying it. She was, and still is, a lovely girl. We went out together for several months."

"So this was a serious relationship?"

"It was on my part. Like most young girls of that age, Babs was a bit flirtatious. All the boys liked her. She was very pretty and she had a good figure."

"So you had some competition from other lads. The Greenhalgh brothers for example?"

"She was close to Kevin for some time and I suspect Carlton was interested, despite their age gap, even in those days."

"When Babs returned to the village after her mother's death did you resume the friendship?

"I was tempted but I wasn't good enough for her. She had her eye on Carlton. I could see why. I live in a fairly pokey house and Carlton owned a bloody mansion. He was married to Elizabeth but that didn't stop him getting in there."

"Did you get the impression the two of them were in a close relationship?"

"They certainly messed around together. Everyone was

aware of that. I wasn't exactly confided in. I've no idea how genuine they were."

"Were you jealous of Carlton and his friendship with Babs?"

"So this is where all these questions have been leading? I admit I hoped Babs and I could pick up from our schooldays. Carlton was a lot older and I suppose he was a more attractive catch than me, married or not. He had money to splash around. I'm not saying Babs was mercenary but he certainly had more to offer than I had."

"I asked if you were jealous of their relationship?" DCI Yates repeated.

"Yes, I was, but not enough to kill the man. All's fair in love and war, so they say. I was, am, very keen on Babs Slater. Unfortunately, she doesn't seem to feel the same. But we are still on good terms. I had very little to do with Carlton. I didn't like him even before Babs returned. He was a bum – too full of himself. But he was clever and he'd made a success of his business life. Though I think he married the wrong woman. I doubt if he and Elizabeth were very compatible. I never married myself."

The DCI turned to Harry Barnes, "Do you have any questions for Mr Brown, Sergeant?"

Harry was unprepared for the query. He looked up from the notes he'd been diligently taking. "I don't think so, Sir," he replied, but he was pleased the DCI had consulted him.

"In that case, you can go, Bradley. Thank you for your co-operation. We'll probably need to speak to you again at some point."

Bradley wiped his brow as he left the room. For him, it had been an ordeal. He had not expected to be questioned on his personal life so closely. It seems nothing is sacred where murder is concerned and the cops had treated him with respect. He saw Dougie waiting in the reception area but pretended not to notice him and walked straight out of the Police Station as quickly as his legs could carry him.

For his part, Dougie was too busy protesting to Police Constable Greg Thomas about being kept waiting to notice the golfer leaving. A further fifteen minutes elapsed before the investigating officers called DougieWatson into the interview room. They had spent that time planning how to approach the Golf Professional with the facts they had uncovered.

DCI Yates began by thanking Dougie for coming in.

"I hope it's not too inconvenient a time for you, Mr Watson?" he said.

"No time's convenient. I've a busy shop to run and it's mid-season. Players are eager to book times. We're nearly always up to our eyes."

"If you take a seat we'll try to get this over with as fast as we can. Some evidence has been discovered which needs clarifying. We're almost certain you can help us,"

"Fire away." Dougie took the seat facing the two officers across the desk.

"Yesterday, you were among those who came in to give a DNA sample."

"So what? You asked for it."

"The lab have come up with an interesting result. Apparently, you share your DNA with another member of Fisborough Golf Club. Do you have any idea who that might be?"

"I was expecting this. I'd be daft to say no, wouldn't I? I guess it's Bab's Slater. We're related but why does that concern you?"

"You're an intelligent man. We're investigating a murder."

"In that case I assume you've also discovered I have a DNA connection with the victim. We were related, too."

DCI Yates's face remained impassive but Harry Barnes gave a gasp.

"So you've found out. Babs Slater is my mother and Carlton Greenhalgh was my father."

"Would you like to start at the beginning, Mr Watson. We have confirmed that Ms Slater gave birth to a child when she was just fifteen and that the child was adopted."

"I only recently traced Babs. The couple who adopted me led me to believe I was their child. My adoptive parents were in their late forties when I joined them. I'd a happy enough childhood but I always knew things weren't quite right. Call it intuition. Alex Watson died two years ago and his wife Flora at the beginning of this year. I learned of my adoption only after they were both dead."

"And you set about tracing your birth mother?"

"Their lawyer handed over what details he had and I traced Babs Slater through the internet. It wasn't difficult and there was a tearful reunion about six months ago. Babs was happy to meet me but she wasn't prepared to go public. Not yet anyway. At the time I had been working as the professional at the Adenbridge Course in East Sussex. She told me she played golf at Fisborough and that John More, Fisborough's professional, was on the move. I applied for the job and got it without my mother having to divulge our connection. Apart from my father no-one else had any idea of our relationship."

DCI Yates listened to Dougie Watson's revelation intently.

"How did you come to understand Carlton Greenhalgh was your father?"

"Bab's told me when I first came here. I was surprised to

discover they were involved with each other again."

"Were you happy about that?"

"Carlton was the last man I'd want to be my parent. I didn't like him and he showed no sign of liking me, either. I can't stand the fact that Edward is my half-brother. Fortunately, he doesn't know that. He's such a prat."

"And the appeal you made to Mr Greenhalgh for a thousand pounds. That wasn't for purchases was it?"

"No, but it was my due. He'd paid nothing towards my keep as a child. I thought it was time he contributed and I'd run up a few debts. Needed the money."

DCI Yates twiddled with a pen between his fingers and shuffled some of his papers around.

"Had you ever considered Carlton Greenhalgh might not be your father?"

"Of course not. Babs was quite clear about that. She was very honest with me. She was just a kid when she had me. He was twice her age. He should have been more responsible. He took advantage of her. Babs is a good woman and life hasn't been very kind to her. I hoped to change that, but not while she was tied up with Carlton Greenhalgh."

"What if I were to tell you I was informed this morning that your DNA is not compatible with that of Mr Greenhalgh. That he is not related to you in any way."

Dougie visibly paled. "Are you serious? But Babs …."

"She was mistaken. It is possible she truly believed he was your father."

"Then who the hell is? Do you know? Does Babs know anything about this?"

"Not yet, on both counts. We decided to hear your story first. You do realise all this may have a bearing on our investigation into Greenhalgh's murder? We'll be rechecking your previous statements very carefully. It would help if you have someone who can confirm you went to the toilets when you left the shop on Sunday morning after you'd been speaking to your mother."

"Graham knows I went?"
"He can vouch for you leaving the shop. That's all. Did you speak to anyone else? Did anyone see you go into the toilets?"

"How the blazes do I know? I wasn't paying any attention to other people. At that time it was pretty quiet. Most players don't come that early on a Sunday, and those that do were already out on the course. How the hell was I to know I'd need witnesses?"

"Right, Mr Watson. Is there anything else at all you want to tell us?"

"Haven't I said enough? If you're thinking of pinning this crime on me, think again. I had nothing to do with that man's death, I swear."

"We would appreciate it if you don't contact your mother before we've had a chance to explain to her. She is bound to be affected by what we tell her and we have been trained to handle these situations."

Dougie agreed and left the station with a lot on his mind and the knowledge that DCI Yates would want to see him again.

Originally they had intended to detain the Golf Professional until they had spoken to Babs Slater. The latter had phoned in to ask if she could come in the afternoon as the delivery she'd been expecting hadn't arrived. DCI Yates confirmed that would be in order. Now, having interviewed her son, he was glad to have a break before speaking to Ms Slater. He conferred with Harry as between them they compiled a report on the morning's findings.

Lunch was spent in the tiny canteen and the DCI and his Sergeant discussed everything other than the case as both settled for potato and leek soup and a bacon sandwich. Refreshed, they returned to the interview room to await Babs Slater. She arrived slightly out of breath and apologising profusely. The delivery man had been running well behind schedule.

DCI Yates invited her to take a seat and asked PC Thomas to organise coffee, despite the fact he and Harry had already had two mugs full with their lunch. Harry was convinced Yates had a soft spot for Ms Slater and this was confirmed when he began his questioning, his tone much more gentle than that which he had employed when speaking to Elizabeth Greenhalgh, Bradley Brown and Dougie Watson.

"Thank you for coming. As you know we have to ask questions and they are not always easy ones to answer. We have made some progress with our inquiries and certain of the facts we've revealed concern you. I'm sorry if what we have to tell you is upsetting. You were good enough to disclose details of your life in Fisborough as a young girl and open enough to tell us you left to stay with an aunt in Sussex, having become pregnant at the age of fifteen."

Babs nodded. She fidgeted as she wondered what the Police Officer was going to say next.

"This morning we spoke to Dougie Watson, Fisborough Golf Club's Professional. As you are aware yesterday you and a number of other people were called in to give a sample of DNA. The results show that you share your DNA with Mr Watson. This proves the two of you are related. Dougie has confirmed that he is your son and that he had traced you a few months ago. You told him of the vacancy at the Fisborough club, he applied and was successful in becoming the club's professional. Is what we've been told so far correct?"

Babs Slater had listened with increasing discomfort to what was being said. She whispered her reply, "Yes."

"Why didn't you tell us of your close relationship before?"

Babs cleared her throat. "Dougie and I had an agreement to keep our relationship secret for the time being. We were still getting used to it ourselves. I was delighted he had found me. When you give up a child for adoption, you never forget. Never stop regretting things could have been different. I was so young and my parents only thought was to hush up what they saw as my shame. I was in no position to keep a child. I was frightened and at the time adoption seemed my only option. I'm still trying to come to terms with the fact I've been given a second chance to have my son in my life."

"Sorry, it is necessary to ask you this. Who is Dougie's father?"

"Do I need to answer that?"

"Perhaps I can make it easier for you. Dougie has informed us you told him Carlton Greenhalgh fathered him."

"Yes, I'm sure of it."

"In that case this might come as a shock. The DNA we have obtained proves conclusively that this is not the case. Carlton Greenhalgh is not Dougie's father. Can you tell us who could be?"

Babs Slater buried her head in her hands and wept. DCI Yates waited patiently for her to recover her composure. He handed her a tissue and she blew her nose vigorously.

"I really did believe it was Carlton. You're right. This has come as a tremendous shock. I wasn't really a promiscuous young girl. I was growing up and I suppose you could call it experimenting. When you are in your teens your sexual feelings are strong but you don't understand how easy it is to conceive. That sounds odd when so many married couples find it difficult. The pregnancy wasn't straightforward and the birth left me sterile but I wasn't to find that out until after I married some years later. If I'd been told that immediately I'm sure I'd have found some way to keep Richard – that was my name for Dougie."

"So you had sexual relations with lads other than Carlton at that time?"

"It sounds awful but I was seeing Carlton's brother Kevin and Bradley Brown at the time. Brad and I only got together twice, though."

DCI Yates said, "That must have been enough. If your child was Kevin Greenhalgh's, Carlton would have still been a contender as they would have DNA in common."

"And what about Bradley's swab? I guess it was compatible?"

"Bradley's results are not known to us yet. But from what you say, there can be little doubt he is Dougie Watson's genetic father."

"Oh, my God, Bradley? I can't believe it and all these years I was so sure it was Carlton. Physically Bradley and Dougie have nothing in common except perhaps their hair. I can't believe it. Bradley Brown."

Babs had stopped crying and was trying to come to grips with what she'd learned. There had been no one else in her life at that time so she had no doubts in her mind.

"We understand this is a big shock to you. Are you all right? Would you like to speak with one of our counsellors?"

Babs assured Yates she would be fine.

"No doubt you and Bradley will have a lot to discuss, but

I must advise you to wait until we have confirmed the result from Bradley's DNA."

"You realise Ms Slater, this could have some bearing on the case. We will continue our investigation and see what emerges."

"If you suspect Bradley Brown of killing Carlton, I'm sure you are wrong. He couldn't kill a fly and as for Dougie … he thought Carlton was his father and he'd only just found him. I know they didn't hit it off at first but given time they would have."

"It's our job to find Carlton Greenhalgh's murderer however unpleasant the solution. We will almost certainly have to speak to you again, Ms Slater, but thank you for your assistance so far."

Still looking somewhat bewildered Babs stood up, shook hands with the officers and went home.

"She took that better than I expected," Harry Barnes said.

"It will just be sinking in. You know, I like that woman. I'm pretty sure she isn't guilty of Greenhalgh's murder. I only hope she doesn't have to face more upsetting news. You do see that this places her son, and Bradley Brown, in more prominent roles on the suspects list. I wonder what Babs told Dougie about her meeting with Greenhalgh that morning? Did she let slip he had slapped her face? Dougie is a young, powerful guy used to swinging a club. The time he was away from the shop would be tight but he could have done it. He could have been the man Martin says he saw. We know he disliked Carlton. Let's hope for his sake someone witnessed him going into the gent's toilets."

"So what do we look at next?"

"With a bit of luck we'll get a quick response from the lab on Bradley's DNA swab. Then we'll know for sure who's the daddy. Maybe Babs Slater was involved with others and has had a lapse of memory. Stringing three young men along at the same time was some going, especially for those days."

Harry admitted to being flummoxed and his superior agreed.

"We may have gathered more information but nothing is any clearer. I need to make out a report for Detective Superintendent Carter. Reckon I'll go home, put on some background music and see if the muse settles on my shoulder. I could do with some inspiration."

"And tomorrow?"

"We need to back-track again. Go over every tiny detail. Try to see if we've missed anything. Are you getting disillusioned with all this crime investigation stuff, Harry?"

"Not at all. It's different from the usual routine. I'll see if I can come up with any new ideas."

"Talking of fresh ideas, have any of the boys turned up trumps?"

"Greg has collected a file of stuff from some of the minor follow ups. He's due to hand it to me before the end of his shift."

"Well, that's your bedtime reading for tonight. I don't suppose Sheenagh has reported anything?"

"Not as far as I know."

"Okay, I'm off. See you in the morning and I'll have a plan of action by then."

***

Although comfortably seated in his own lounge, Raymond Yates sighed as he continued to seek some clue that would bring the Greenhalgh case nearer to a conclusion. Fisborough Golf Club had certainly turned out to be a hornet's nest. He found himself contemplating how many other clubs, golf, rugby, cricket, bridge, poker and more, hid such a plethora of intrigue.

"Oh, what a tangled web…" he quoted aloud to himself before tuning into Radio Classic to seek out a soothing background for his thoughts.

His mother interrupted his evening again to tell him the party plans had been put in motion.

"Have you invited Karen yet?"

"Sorry, Mum, I've had other important things on my mind."

"It's always the same. Surely you can switch off sometimes? Neglect your social life and you'll regret it later in life when you're facing a lonely old age."

Yates had heard it all before. He supposed his mother had a point. He rarely managed to switch off to pursue a private life. If he were honest, there were times when he didn't think he wanted to. Investigating crime was his life and it was interesting enough to be totally absorbing. On the other hand he was fond of Karen and she deserved better from him. He promised to phone her at the weekend and appease his mother for another couple of days.

The revelation that Carlton wasn't Dougie's father had thrown him. He'd almost accepted it as an established fact. Babs Slater had appeared so positive. It was yet another reminder of the constant need to keep an open mind on everything. With that, he resumed his trawl through the evidence they'd accrued for the umpteenth time. He reached the point where Callum Martin had reported seeing Babs Slater and Carlton Greenhalgh apparently arguing and recalled Harry pointing out that the fellow hadn't called in at the station to give his DNA swab. He made a note to chase Martin up and added it to the schedule for the following day.

Closing his folders and turning off the radio, he climbed

into bed, wishing he could solve the case during his sleep. Unfortunately any dreams he might have had were forgotten by the morning.

CHAPTER 9

Saturday dawned brightly. DCI Yates met Sergeant Barnes at the Station and they adjourned to the canteen for coffee and bacon rolls. Harry Barnes had already knuckled down to work and was eager to let his Chief know.

"I've reminded Callum Martin to call in for his DNA swab," he imparted between bites of his roll.

"You must have been reading my last night's thoughts. I'd placed his name top of the day's agenda. It's a mere formality but one we shouldn't neglect. Did he say why he didn't turn up the other day?"

"He was a bit vague. Claimed it had slipped his mind and blamed senile dementia."

"I guess he is getting on."

"Seventy–three to be precise."

"Oh well, we'll expect him this morning. Is there any word on Bradley's DNA results?"

"I'll check with Pauline."

"Thanks," the DCI finished his coffee and replaced the cup on the table. "Young Dougie came over pretty well yesterday. He opened up nicely and appeared more relaxed now that his secret has been exposed."

Harry nodded. "I can understand why he and Babs Slater wanted to keep it under wraps. He seemed genuinely surprised Carlton wasn't his father."

"And, in a way, I believe he was relieved. He didn't like the victim or his son, that's for sure."

Yates and Barnes binned their waxed paper plates and returned to Harry's cramped office.

"So what now?" Harry asked.

Detective Chief Inspector Yates ran his hand through his hair. "I'm not decided where to...." He began before the shrill ring of the phone interrupted him in mid stream.

"DCI Yates speaking. Mike, I hoped you'd get in touch.... You have?...Really, that's settled then. Thanks." Yates replaced the phone and faced Harry Barnes. "DNA Department. Seems Babs Slater was telling the truth about her boyfriends. Bradley Brown is Dougie's father. No more speculating required."

"Will we let Babs break the news?"

"No, Harry. I fancy a trip to Fisborough Golf Club this morning. We'll tell Dougie who's his daddy and watch the reaction. We need to show our face again. Keep them all guessing. And you never know what other titbits we'll uncover."

"Right, I'll just let the men know where to find us."

***

Agnes came forward to greet them as they entered the dining lounge.

"Coffees?" she queried.

"Not at the moment, thanks. How did your quiz night go?"

"Very busy. A lot more people than usual turned up. Who says crime doesn't pay? We boosted the club's profits. Of course, there was a lot of chat about Carlton's murder at first but it was good to see the members and their guests enjoying themselves as they joined in the quiz. Half the profits go to charity so we weren't the only ones to benefit from the good turnout."

The DCI moved towards the full length windows and looked out to the Professional's Shop. Harry followed his gaze but kept the conversation general.

"Seems as if everything's getting back to normal. Agnes appeared more composed than she did previously. I'm often amazed how quickly people can move on from a tragedy."

"That's true if you're not too deeply involved. But someone has to be shivering in their shoes still." DCI Yates averted his gaze to the family room as Agnes passed by carrying plates of food. He stopped her in her tracks, "I see you've opened the curtains. I guess you needed the space for the quiz."

"You can still use it, though," Agnes said.

"Good, I'll get Jack Davis to ask Dougie Watson to come through if it's possible."

Jack Davis was only too pleased to help and the investigating officers found a seat in the family room. With the curtains still open, they could see Dougie talking to his assistant outside the shop as Jack approached. Dougie glanced through the windows to where the officers were seated, then, with a few words to Graham, he followed Jack through to the family room.

"Good morning, Dougie." Both officers greeted the club professional. The DCI noted Jack Davis was still hovering near their table. "If you don't mind Jack we want a private word with Mr Watson."

The steward moved away looking slightly embarrassed and wandered off behind the bar. Confident they could no longer be overheard, DCI Yates addressed DougieWatson.

"I thought you deserved to know what the DNA results have thrown up."

Dougie paled, "They can't have found any evidence to connect me to Carlton's murder. I didn't do it."

"It's not that. We now know who your real father is."

Dougie Watson paled even further. "I'm not sure I want to know. Have you told Babs?"

"She's not been informed officially yet, but we are fairly certain she's worked it out for herself."

Dougie braced himself, "Come on then, spill the beans, who is it? Do I know him?"

Detective Chief Inspector Yates looked directly at Dougie Watson as he spoke. "Hope this isn't too much of a shock. It's Bradley Brown."

Dougie sat back in his chair, "You're kidding. Bradley Brown? You mean he and Babs….?"

"The pair of them were in a relationship at the same time she was going out with Carlton and his brother," the DCI explained. "I'm sure she'll fill in the details when she sees you."

"Babs and Bradley. It's common knowledge he fancies her, but all that time ago…It's hard to take in."

"Can I get you a drink?" Harry Barnes offered. "It's obvious this has come as a shock."

"No thanks. Babs and Bradley," Dougie repeated. "You know what? I'd rather have Brad as my dad than Carlton and thank God I'm not related to Edward. Does Brad know?"

"Not yet. We'll be telling him shortly, however, I expect the three of you will want to get together at some point. Would you like me to arrange with Mr Winter for you to have the remainder of today off? I could come up with a reason."

"I'd rather get back to the shop. I've a few jobs to see to. I'll be fine, but I'd sooner no-one else knows until I get a chance to talk to my mother. If that's all, I'll get back to work now. I was about to do the accounts."

"If you're absolutely sure you're okay, then you're free to go." The DCI shook Dougie's hand and the professional headed for the patio doors and his shop. Harry Barnes noted Jack Davis watching inquisitively from behind the bar as Dougie left.

"There'll be a lot of tongues wagging when this news gets out," the Sergeant said. DCI Yates concurred.

The two men sat for a while looking out over the first fairway. Marion Chapman and Philippa Hawksworth were teeing off.

"One day," Yates said, "You and I are going to get a game, Harry, I promise. It will be our reward for solving this wretched case."

The officers were about to pack up when James Winter approached them.

"Good morning. How's progress, or shouldn't I be asking?"

"Shaping up nicely," Yates replied. "Had you something to tell us?"

"I'm afraid not. Unless you want to arrest that man Martin for harassment. He's accosted several members to support his application for membership. He even had the cheek to come into my office earlier and suggest that he should fill the vacancy caused by Carlton's departure. He stressed that we couldn't deny a place was available. When I told him he wasn't first on the waiting list he exploded. Seems to think he should have priority. When I tell the Board about this episode I doubt if he'll ever be granted his wish."

The officers could tell how rattled the club secretary was and Harry Barnes sympathised with him,

"Callum Martin's not exactly our favourite person just now either. He failed to turn up when we took the DNA swabs the other day and we had to chase him."

They left James Winter and returned to the Fisborough police station as Callum Martin was leaving.

"Talk of the devil," Harry commented.

DCI Yates addressed Martin with a degree of sarcasm. "Glad you could make it this time around."

Callum Martin muttered something about the inconvenience and went on to rave about Fisborough Golf Club before heading down the road.

"Miserable old bugger," Harry observed and Yates nodded in agreement.

"More important things for us to worry about," he said.

The DCI decided to remain at the station whilst he sent two women police officers to tell Babs the news she already suspected. Bradley Brown had fathered her son. At the same time, Harry and Greg Thomas were dispatched to break the news of the DNA results to Bradley Brown.

"Me? Dougie Watson's father?" Bradley was in tears. "Babs and I had a son together all those years ago and I never knew? I can't believe it. I heard the rumours at the time but it was just gossip. I never even knew Babs had a son. He was adopted, you say, and she believed Carlton was the father? Are you sure you're not mistaken?"

"The DNA is conclusive."

"Have you told Babs?"

"She's aware of the situation, yes."

"We did get together a couple of times. We were just kids really. You know what it's like. Oh, my God. Dougie Watson. He's a fine strapping lad. I always wanted a son but I never married."

Sergeant Barnes and PC Thomas left Bradley Brown to

come to terms with his newly confirmed status. They got the impression that once he recovered from the shock Bradley would be pleased with his role.

***

DCI Yates was brooding over his files when Sergeant Barnes returned to the office. He looked up.

"So how did he take it?" he asked.

"Pretty well. He was a bit overwhelmed but apparently he's always wanted a son," Harry replied, pulling up a chair beside his senior officer. "What are you looking so perplexed about?

"Everything I guess," DCI Yates sighed. "This is proving a difficult nut to crack. We could compile a good case against several people."

"Want to toss the evidence about between us? I understand it sometimes helps."

"You're learning fast, Harry. We can give it a try. Let's begin with Babs Slater. She's confirmed Martin's evidence that she was with Greenhalgh shortly before he was found dead. She admits they had some sort of argument, though she denies the face slapping. The big question is did she strike the man with his own golf club?"

"She knew how to handle a club but was it possible she had the strength to inflict those wounds to his skull?" Harry Barnes interposed.

"Reports suggest that's unlikely."

"And from what we've surmised of her from our interviews, I would say such violence was completely out of character."

"But who knows what people are capable of if they are pushed beyond the norm? We have no idea of knowing what he said to her. We do know she was upset and that she went and spoke to her son. Could the pair of them have acted together? Dougie does appear to have had the opportunity and if his mother had been slapped and humiliated who knows how he might have reacted. He's a strong lad."

"He's admitted to us he didn't like Carlton. This might have been the straw that led him to have it out with the victim."

"The timescale is very tight. He'd have to be a callous beast to act normally after such an attack and you'd expect a bit of blood would have found its way on to his person. He hadn't changed his clothing."

"Those blows were inflicted from behind, it's possible the perpetrator escaped getting splattered."

"True. And his clothing wasn't examined immediately. That sounds remiss but we had no reason to suspect the guy at the time and in any case he was left alone with the body for a while. He could claim any contamination we might have discovered occurred at that time. There is hard evidence pointing to Watson, however, in the form of that letter we found"

"Yes, and he lied about it at first by saying it concerned purchases from his shop."

"He seemed to think he had a right to the money. Was this refuted by Greenhalgh?"

"That will never be known unless some more evidence turns up."

The DCI sighed, "I'm afraid the young professional has to remain high on our list of suspects but I think we can safely disregard Babs Slater unless she acted with him, of course. I don't think anything showed on Carlton's computer regarding the demand, but we'll check that out again. Let's move on to his new daddy."

"Bradley Brown's statement says he found the body by

chance lying in the rough. He certainly displayed signs of being extremely shocked at his discovery. Shocked enough to throw up."

"Could his claim to have found the body be a cover? He was known to have the hots for Babs Slater. It's possible he witnessed the incident between her and Greenhalgh and confronted the victim after Babs had left. Could he have been so angered as to strike out? It certainly appeared to be an impulsive, passionate act."

"There was a big difference between Greenhalgh and Brown physically. The former was a lot taller and stronger."

"But the attack was from behind. The mystery is how the assailant got hold of the five iron. We have to presume Greenhalgh was carrying it. Someone took it from him or he handed it to them. If it had been grabbed from behind, surely he would have instinctively turned round?"

"You would think so, wouldn't you? And what would have induced him to hand anyone his club?"

"If Bradley Brown committed the offence you would have to think it was to do with Carlton's relationship with Babs Slater. Yet to all intents and purposes he passively accepted that she'd chosen to link up with Greenhalgh."

"Do you think it's likely that such a mild mannered fellow could be capable of murder?"

"Given the right circumstances it's possible. Brown could have been intensely jealous of the Slater/Greenhalgh affair. He could have been envious of everything about the victim. Of his business success, his prestigious house, his position within Fisborough Golf Club itself. Or another motive we haven't hit on yet. Let's take a look closer to home and examine the victim's family."

"Most murders that happen have a family connection."

"That's very true. Elizabeth Greenhalgh is quite a

formidable woman. She's tall and strong. She comes over as cold and intelligent, yet like her husband, she has established a position for herself at the club. You don't become Lady Vice Captain without gaining the respect of most of the members."

"I'm not sure that's necessarily correct. I've heard once you get on the committee it's often purely a case of climbing the ladder."

"Okay, but it's a fact Mrs Greenhalgh lied to us initially about being at the golf course on the morning of her husband's demise."

"I suppose she thought no-one had noted her presence and she didn't want her reason for being there to be divulged."

"Undoubtedly, she thought she could get away with it, but there was always the chance she'd have been spotted. It was possible she had seen Carlton and Babs Slater head for the practice area. Could she have been hovering under cover of the trees and confronted him when Babs left? Why? She already was au fait with their affair and was confident it would fizzle out."

"What if she felt the affair compromised her standing in the club? She's a proud woman."

"Proud enough to try to keep her own dalliance with Grant Mason under wraps. Carlton must have known they went to the concert hall together. His son did. Assumedly, as Grant was supposed to be his friend, he thought there was nothing in it other than their interest in classical music."

"Or it didn't bother him. Maybe he regarded it as useful that Grant kept Elizabeth amused from time to time."

"Perhaps her feelings towards Grant run deeper than she's admitted. Did she regard her husband as an obstacle standing in the way of any future with her lover?"

"But, according to Mrs Greenhalgh, she and Grant Mason were not lovers except in a cultural sense."

"Why would he ask her to go away with him if their relationship wasn't that close?"

"But she hadn't accepted that invite. It seems she wasn't sure she wanted to destroy her cosy lifestyle. Financially she was well provided for."

"But she benefits even more from his death. As his widow, she's entitled to the house and a share of the cash. She's a very wealthy woman."

"But I would surmise she was prior to his death."

"We agree she had the physical strength and ability to wield that club and it would appear she had the opportunity and time. But did she have a strong enough motive? We'll look at her son next. On the surface he might have had a stronger case for killing his father."

"He's been quite open about how he regarded Carlton."

"Most people, whether they liked him or not, thought of Carlton Greenhalgh as a figure of strength and influence. He was the immediate past captain, had a powerful business life and an ego to match, if we believe what we've been told. The one area of his life that could be regarded as unsatisfactory was his marriage. Elizabeth Greenhalgh has implied they were both happy to have a strings free relationship and, of course, Greenhalgh had his little bit on the side, as they say, but for his son , that was his weakness, and his son hated him for it. Was that hatred deep enough to lead Edward to kill?"

"Edward recently married and is expecting a baby. His feelings on fidelity could well have been magnified. He is very close to his mother. Did he feel she was humiliated by his father's blatantly overt relationship with Babs Slater? After all it was clubhouse gossip. Had he found it too embarrassing to ignore? The time factor doesn't look good, but did he lose the rag when he spotted Babs and Carlton together? Did he, in fact, lose more than his golfing partner at the fourteenth? Did he also lose his temper?"

"He was known to have a foul temper when he wasn't playing well. It would be interesting to find out if he were on his game that day, or was his mood already somewhat frayed?"

"I got the feeling that although he didn't exactly disapprove of his mother going out with Grant Mason, he blamed his father for what he might have seen as his parents' marriage falling apart. His wife's father is the local vicar and would no doubt be dismayed if it came to a divorce. That might have reflected on Edward in his in-laws eyes."

"Edward is proud to the extent he is seen as arrogant, like his father, perhaps. However, his apparent aloofness could stem from embarrassment at his dad's behaviour."

"That in itself isn't a hugely strong motive for murder but just supposing he had an inkling about Dougie and Babs. Perhaps he had sensed Dougie might be his father's son, his half-brother. That really would have sent feathers flying, even though as it happens, it's not true."

"But you have nothing to substantiate that. It's all conjecture."

"You're right, of course. I'm just searching for another angle. We can't dismiss Grant Mason from the equation, either. Elizabeth was hesitating about joining him in America. With his own marriage scheduled to be dissolved, Carlton was in his eyes, perhaps the only one obstacle to a life of bliss with Elizabeth."

"I doubt if many people would describe Elizabeth Greenhalgh as someone likely to inspire bliss"

"Love is blind, Harry."

"I've heard that one before. Somehow I can't see Mason as a murderer except on stage playing the part of MacDuff or whoever it was who killed Macbeth."

"Whatever, I'd like to have a further chat with both him and Edward. The latter's been keeping a low profile."

"Could be grieving."

"A likely story, in my opinion. So who else should we be considering?"

"Only, as you once said, over six hundred club members."

"It's a thought, isn't it? I suppose we should still keep Nick Bateman in mind and that fellow Martin's not out of the picture. I think it's safe to dismiss Marion, and Philippa can safely be ruled out, and I don't see Sheenagh, Agnes and Josie as likely candidates. Jack Davis, on the other hand omitted to tell us about his walk with the dog initially. It does give him a window of opportunity and he disliked Greenhalgh but it's not motive enough for murder. I think that just about covers everyone."

"So, do you reckon that little exercise helped?" Harry asked.

"On the surface, not a lot, but it has cleared my mind to a certain extent. It's still open, of course."

Over the next few days the investigation trod water. The team continued to ask questions and dig around at Fisborough Golf Club but new clues were proving elusive. The DNA department had come up with nothing of importance from their examination of Carlton's clothing. A further look at the murder weapon, however, showed up the faintest trace of petrol on the grip. Had Carlton, or anyone of those on the possible suspects list filled their car that morning. It was a mere snippet of info' but the DCI felt it should be followed up, if only to keep the investigating team busy. He put Greg Thomas in charge of making inquiries. There was only one garage anywhere near the clubhouse, which should help make the task easier to find out about customers. That trace's significance could amount to nothing, but one never knew.

WPC Pauline Fergus's trawl through Greenhalgh's computer had again failed to reveal a reply to Dougie's request for money but he could, of course, have sent a handwritten answer or even responded in person. Dougie Watson implied he hadn't received a reply. It seemed, too, Carlton Greenhalgh had confined his interest in soft porn to the magazines under his bed. There was no sign of him seeking it out on the internet.

Mid-week saw DCI Yates heading to a conference with Detective Superintendent Carter. Left to his own devices Harry decided another trip to Fisborough Golf Club was on the cards. If nothing else, he could have a chat with Sheenagh Davis. He timed his visit to coincide with lunch.

"Any chance of some of your delicious macaroni cheese?" he asked Sheenagh.

"I think we can manage that," the steward's wife smiled. "Might take a few minutes to produce, though. We're very busy. There's a party in from the village."

"So I see. Is that Callum Martin with them?"

"It is indeed. Much to Mr Winter's displeasure. Apparently, Mr Martin sent a letter to the Board stirring things up. In fact it's been quite a morning. Elizabeth Greenhalgh was in and raised a few eyebrows by meeting up with Grant Mason. So soon after her husband's death, too. Edward arrived and there was an argument. I tell you it's been all go. To crown it, it's Agnes' day off, so there's only me and Josie, and she's complaining about a sore leg."

"So you're up against it, eh?"

"You can say that again. I'd better get back to the kitchen before the party are ready for their next course."

Harry grinned to himself. Sheenagh was in his opinion a typical woman. Always ready to gossip.

He thought about what she had said. Elizabeth and Grant already in the open and Edward voicing disapproval. Had the mother and her boyfriend colluded to bring about Carlton's demise? It was definitely a possibility. Edward, too, wasn't out of the picture. What they needed was hard evidence and it was in short supply.

The village party had taken over the whole of the family room but it wasn't curtained off. Harry was seated near to the partition. His eye caught that of Callum Martin, who glowered back. James Winter chose that moment to enter the dining room and made towards Harry's table.

"Okay if I join you?" he asked, pulling up a chair and giving Harry Barnes little option but to assent.

"I hear Callum Martin's been giving you a hard time?" Harry said.

"Not just me. That man really is obnoxious. I'd like him banned from the premises. It disturbs me to see him sitting over there but he's obviously part of that party and party bookings bring in money for the club."

"So who are the party?"

"It's the village Historical Society. Since he bought that house and renovated it he's wormed his way into a number of local organisations and considers he should have automatic entrance to this club even though we have a waiting list. Several of our members have complained of being accosted by him on the golf course."

"Accosted by him?"

"That's right. He hops over his garden wall and tries to intimidate members to support his application for inclusion.

We could sue him for trespassing but the general feeling is he's just an old guy with a bee in his bonnet and the club doesn't want any more bad publicity. He claims his brother is the sub-editor of a newspaper and could take up his cause."

"Sounds as if you have a problem with him."

"It's been going on for nearly two years, now. If Carlton Greenhalgh were here he'd be able to fill you in. He was Captain when he first applied and there was a lot of aggro' at the time."

"So, Martin didn't get along with Carlton?"

"I doubt if they ever met in person and they wouldn't have had much to do with each other since Carlton relinquished office, but I'm aware he bombarded Carlton with emails last year, but membership is a matter for the whole Board. It isn't up to the Captain."

"I don't suppose he's shown any sign of violence?"

"Shouldn't think the blundering old fool would go that far. He's aggressive, yes, but he's all talk. He doesn't seem to understand he's doing his cause no good. I wouldn't be surprised if the Board decide to prevent him from ever joining us. Funnily enough, Carlton Greenhalgh expressed some support for the man, though heaven knows why. We could certainly do without his nonsense just now. There's enough on our plate."

"Quite right," Harry commented, thoughtfully, before steering the conversation into calmer waters until James Winter left when Sheenagh arrived with Harry's macaroni and cheese and a side plate of chips.

"So was Mr Winter going on about Callum Martin?" Sheenagh asked.

"He was indeed," Barnes confirmed.

"Mr Martin does go on a lot but, you know, I've some

sympathy for him, along with a number of others. His house is practically sitting on the course. I can see why he wants to be a member. But, as my Jack says, rules are rules and he'll need to wait his turn like everybody else."

Sergeant Barnes ate his lunch in silence. He mulled over what he had learned and noted the need to look into some points. Did this give Callum Martin more prominence on the list of suspects? Hardly, if Carlton had been on his side in the argument, but was he aware of that?

Wild goose chase or not it was worth a follow up. He wondered if Carlton Greenhalgh's computer still stored any of those emails. It would be worth ordering a search. He'd get young Pauline on to it. She was already familiar with the machine and was always eager to be given a job other than accompanying other officers whilst they led what ever enquiry it was they were working on. One day she'd rise up the ranks if she didn't marry her rugby player and bury herself in nappies.

***

Harry lingered round the Golf Club for the next hour or two. He dropped in at the professional shop and asked Dougie if he was prepared to tell him what Babs had said about her meeting with Carlton prior to his being found dead.

"You've already heard that from her I gather. My mother is a good woman, I tell you. There's no way she'd have harmed Greenhalgh. She believed she loved him and she's hurting right now."

"Sorry, but we do have to repeat some of our queries even if you find it annoying. Have you discovered anyone who saw you actually going into the toilets after she left?"

"No, I haven't. You have only my word for it. I did not go over to the practice area and club my mother's lover to death. But I could have. I didn't like the man and I've made no secret of that, but there's no way you're going to pin what happened to Greenhalgh on me."

Maybe you're right, Harry Barnes thought to himself, but he was remembering his boss' advice to keep an open mind at all times.

Back at the station a message from DCI Yates told him his chief wouldn't be home until the following evening around seven. He would appreciate a call after that time.

Harry decided it was in order for him to knock off a little early and join his sons in a game of football. Mary would appreciate seeing him for a while, too. Recently it had been all work and no play. Before he left he told WPC Fergus he had an investigative job lined up for her in the morning.

"Great," the policewomen said. "I'll look forward to it."

She, too, ended her shift and Harry offered her a lift home.

"I'm okay," she said. "Ewan's waiting for me in the Feathers." She crossed over the road and walked towards the popular pub. Harry hoped she'd keep a clear head for her morning shift.

CHAPTER 10

Harry Barnes arrived home to a quiet house. He'd forgotten Mary had told him she was going over to see her sister who lived a couple of streets away and the boys were having a sleepover with their cousins. He resigned himself to no football and decided to order a pizza from Antonio's.

He settled down to watch the news on television while he waited for it to be delivered. For the past few days coverage had died down on the golf course murder apart from a brief mention but possibly because there was little else of local interest a reporter had been dispatched to the club looking for a story.

The bulletin began with a picture of the Fisborough Golf Course and then focussed in on the Club house just as the Historic Society party were leaving. Harry must have missed the cameras by minutes and he wasn't sorry.

A young news man approached two ladies who said they were delighted to see the club getting back to normal. Their meal had been delicious and, although Carlton Greenhalgh's death had been on the tips of many tongues, they had spent an enjoyable afternoon. The ladies agreed it was a tragic thing to have happened and said one of the investigating officers had been in at lunch time continuing with inquiries. The reporter was about to sum up when Callum Martin appeared on the screen. He walked up to the newsman and began to tell them his story.

"I live in that house over there beside the course. You can't see it from this angle. I could tell you a thing or two about the goings on at this club. I've been trying to join since I moved in over two years ago."

The reporter had been taken by surprise by Martin but he listened calmly for a minute or so while the old man ranted and gestured with his stick.

"It's like a closed shop here," he said. "Those detectives aren't likely to get anywhere with this lot and that's a fact."

The broadcast was quickly wound up as he made his point. The newsman concluded by saying he was sure the local force would get to the bottom of the crime before long.

Harry found himself laughing. What did that Martin fellow think he was going to achieve by behaving like that? He'd made a fool of himself standing waving his stick about. Seemed he was hell bent on gaining a bit of the limelight. Winter's was right. The man was a blundering idiot.

His phone rang almost as soon as the news programme finished. DCI Yates had caught the bulletin and was as amused as Harry. "Guess you saw the news? What did you make of that?" he asked.

"Not a lot," Harry replied. "But the old chap had probably had a glass or two of wine with his meal. He has been causing a stir at the club. Seems to think he should inherit Greenhalgh's place on the membership list."

"He does, does he?" Yates laughed. "Enjoy your evening. I'll speak to you tomorrow night to catch up. I've to go for cocktails before dining with the Super and his associates."

"Lucky you," Harry said, replacing the receiver. The doorbell indicated Antonio's pizza had arrived. He placed it on a tray and carried it through to the lounge. With no kids and no Mary to scold him for not sitting at the table, he ate his meal with relish and wondered if the DCI's dinner would be as appetising.

***

The following day Sergeant Barnes allocated the investigation into any possible historic emails from Callum Martin lurking on Carlton Greenhalgh's computer to WPC Fergus and she settled into the task. It wasn't exactly the job she'd hoped for. Several of the officers had seen Martin interrupting the news report and those who hadn't soon heard about it.

"Bet it's also the topic of conversation down at the Golf Club," Greg Thomas observed. "By the way I had another word with Nick Baker but he didn't have anything to add to his previous statement."

"Thanks for that."

"The Club Captain, Clive Meechan, made a point of asking me what was happening. He'd been away for a few days. He seemed a bit put out that we hadn't been clamouring to keep him informed."

"I suppose as Captain the guy might expect us to notify him of any major developments, but if he's not been around we couldn't, could we? He hasn't exactly figured in our inquiries. He wasn't playing that morning and had only dropped in later for a chat with his cronies. We've no reason to doubt what he told us. Plenty of folk saw him arrive after twelve and before that he'd been taking the collection at the local church. Unless he conjured up some divine spirit to act for him he had nothing to do with Greenhalgh's tragic end."

Greg grinned. "I hear what you're saying but it's a question of protocol apparently to inform the Captain what's what."

"I know," Harry sighed. "Golf and protocol go hand in glove. We'll draft a brief report to satisfy the chap but it won't give anything away."

"Do we have anything to give away?" Greg asked as he moved out of the office and made for the canteen and his mid-morning break.

Harry Barnes realised not for the first time that the case seemed to be bogged down. They were working hard and deserved a break.

A hint of one came after lunch. Detective Constable Jacobs who had been seconded to supplement the station's force at the start of the case had spent most of his time helping with the routine work. They might have a murder to deal with but they still had to handle the everyday stuff like lost property, driving offences and so on. He had been asked to check out Wilson's the local garage to find out if any known names had called in for petrol the morning of the crime. Two names had come to light. Edward Greenhalgh had filled his tank. According to the garage attendant he'd appeared a bit agitated. He'd asked for a rag to mop up a spillage of petrol that had run down the side of his car.

Jacobs quoted the attendant as saying, "I went out to clean it for him but all he did was complain he was going to be late for his game and he left in a hurry without a word of thanks and only just missed colliding with a van as he drove onto the road."

He distinctly remembered it being about 8.30am because he was due to knock off having been on night shift and he'd had to clean his hands again before going home. Dougie Watson had filled up some time earlier. They'd had a bit of banter about Saturday's football results. The two men were said to be like chalk and cheese in their manner. Edward and Dougie were regulars at the garage and the man knew both of them well. He didn't know if anyone had called in later because he'd gone home.

Sergeant Barnes thanked the detective constable and said he'd pass the report on to the DCI that evening when he returned from the conference. He wasn't sure how important Jacob's information would prove to be. But at least it was information and, having been told about the trace of petrol found on the weapon, it might be the lead they needed. He'd a feeling DCI Yates would be taking it seriously. Barnes considered checking it out with DougieWatson and Edward Greenhalgh immediately but on second thoughts decided to wait for Yates to return to action. After all, Jacobs's report only indicated the two men had both been in contact with a petrol pump that morning. It didn't necessarily mean it was the same brand as the trace found on the blade of the five iron belonging to the victim. In fact the more Harry thought about it the more he became convinced it was probably a red herring. There were always red herrings in the detective novels he read. He was aware he was a novice when it came to investigating anything as serious as murder. At that moment without DCI Yates at his side he felt particularly incompetent.

WPC Fergus was still sitting at the computer when he went through to the duty room.

"Any luck?" he asked.

"Might have," she replied. "I'd some help from one of the other officers but I've managed to retrieve the correspondence you were interested in, or at least some of it. Want to have a look, Sir?"

Harry took a sheaf of emails Pauline had printed out. "There's quite a number of them. Mr Martin certainly expressed himself forcibly."

The sergeant sat down and began to read the mail. It

started off calmly enough but became more aggressive and threatening as time went on. Some of Carlton Greenhalgh's replies were still attached and they showed the then Captain had been controlled in his response to what was quite offensive material at times.

"I think that's all I can find, Sir," the WPC said.

"You've done very well. At the very least they give us some insight into Callum Martin's state of mind and they tell us a bit about Carlton Greenhalgh, too. Thank you and well done."

Pauline looked pleased with her day's work even though she owed Jacobs a pint.

Harry arrived home having been delayed by the woman worried about her missing dog.

Mary greeted him with the words, "Your dinner's ready in the oven. We went ahead and ate. The boys are upstairs doing their homework."

Harry sat down to eat a home made cheese and ham quiche served with creamed potatoes and a generous helping of broccoli. The apple crumble that followed was scrumptious.

"Now you've finished, I'll tell you. DCI Yates phoned a few minutes before you arrived home."

"Why didn't you let me know immediately?" Harry exclaimed, jumping up from the kitchen table to reach for the phone.

"I wanted you to enjoy your meal first. I noticed you only had pizza last night because I was out."

"It was a great pizza," Harry said.

Mary carried the dishes into the kitchen. She knew to keep out of the way when her husband was speaking to DCI Yates.

"Sergeant Barnes here, Sir, I gathered you phoned?"

The voice at the other end sounded bright and refreshed, Harry felt tired and weary.

"Why go all formal on me, Harry? What have you managed to find out in my absence?"

As briefly as possible Harry told him.

"Sounds as if you've been kept busy. It all appears quite interesting, too. We'll need to go over it and see where we stand now. Okay, get a good sleep and we'll catch up tomorrow."

Harry Barnes had expected his Chief to sound more enthusiastic but perhaps his mind wasn't set on the Fisborough Golf Club case after his couple of days with the bigwigs. Well, if Yates was prepared to lay off work, so could he. He went into the lounge and waited for Mary to join him. Upstairs he could hear the boys larking about and it didn't sound as if they were doing homework. He found a good family film on the television and called them to come and watch. Mary appeared with a cup of tea and they settled down to some light entertainment. Carlton Greenhalgh's murder stayed firmly on the back shelf for that entire evening.

CHAPTER 11

Harry felt a sense of relief when he saw DCI Yates sitting in his office ready to start work. The chief was back. Repeating what he'd told him the previous evening and being as concise as he could, he told his superior officer all that had taken place in his absence, beginning with Callum Martin.

"That fellow's name does seem to be cropping up a lot. He's a typical attention seeker. This murder is possibly the most exciting thing in his whole life, and he got on to the telly. Now that's fame."

Yates showed much more interest in Jacobs's report on the garage.

"And this attendant can be regarded as reliable?"

"DC Jacobs thinks so."

"We'll nip down and have a chat with Dougie Watson again. I doubt if Edward will be around till the weekend. Dougie will be able to confirm if he's booked a tee-off time. Any news about when, or if, Grant Mason has finalised plans to go to the States?"

"I don't know but will try to find out. Maybe that was what he was discussing with Elizabeth Greenhalgh when Edward joined them and caused a row."

"It's quite likely," Yates agreed.

Harry finished giving instructions to the officers on duty about a number of routine jobs and sent Jacobs out on the trail of the missing dog. The woman owner had already put in an appearance that morning begging for help. Satisfied his station was under control, he joined DCI Yates and the latter drove them to the Golf Club. At eleven o'clock the clubhouse was quiet. They made their way through the patio doors to the professional's shop where Dougie Watson was helping a golfer choose a new pair of shoes and indicated he wouldn't be long.

With the sale successfully completed, Dougie turned to the two police officers.

"What do you want to know this time?" he asked.

"Just need confirmation of a piece of information passed to us. We've been told that on the morning of Carlton Greenhalgh's murder you stopped at Wilson's Garage for petrol."

Dougie looked puzzled and thought for a minute. "Yes, I did."

"Can you confirm what time that would be?"

"Around seven-thirty. Maybe a tad earlier because I think I was here by half past."

"Thank you, that's all we need to know for the present."

"What the hell has my going to the garage got to do with anything?"

"Just checking," Yates replied, and he and Barnes went back into the clubhouse.

"Damn it," the DCI cursed. "We forgot to find out when Edward's expected to put in an appearance."

"I'll go," Harry offered. He left Yates to conjure up coffee and went back into the shop. Dougie was able to tell him Edward had booked a time for 4pm that evening. He was playing a tie and with it being Friday he could escape his office early."

"Sounds promising," Yates said. "We can come back again then and hopefully get the petrol business over with in the one day."

"Do you think we are clutching at straws?"

"Quite probably, but I'll get Jacobs to check on the type of petrol they both use. If they are regulars the attendant should have a good idea. We could have checked with Dougie but I'm not going to interrupt him again. I'm not completely with it this morning. With any luck one will use four star and the other diesel. The lab indicated the trace belonged to the former."

"I see where you're coming from," Harry said, but he still had a feeling knowing wouldn't help that much.

DCI Yates confided that Detective Superintendent Carter was concerned their enquiries hadn't produced a strong line of procedure yet, He'd said he'd be looking for further developments sooner rather than later.

"I told him we'd been working flat out and he just nodded and advised me we had to keep persevering."

"What the devil does he think we've been doing? Sitting around on our arses drinking cups of tea?"

It was only after he'd said it that Harry acknowledged cups of tea and coffee played a fairly large part in their investigation.

Judging Edward would most likely arrive at the course in plenty of time for his match, the officers put in their second appearance at the club at three-thirty pm to be informed Edward was already in the changing room. When they joined him there he was embarrassed to be caught with his trousers down. He quickly shuffled out of his suit bottoms and replaced them with casuals.

"You do seem to pick the most inconvenient times to

speak to me. I'm about to play in the second round of the Club Championship in less than half an hour."

"We won't hold you back for long. We've been led to believe you stopped at Wilson's garage for petrol on the way to the course on the day of your father's death?"

"What if I did?"

"Well, did you?"

"I don't know, I can't remember... Yes, I did. I recall I was down to my last and wouldn't have had sufficient fuel to drive home. I was late as it was and it was a bloody nuisance but I had to pull in. What has this to do with your inquiries?"

DCI Yates ignored Edward's last question and this time he didn't forget to ask what petrol he used.

"Four Star. I've not switched to diesel though I've thought about it."

"Good, now the attendant told us you managed to spill some petrol down the side of your car."

"That's right and the man took his time mopping it up. It wasn't much and I started wiping it off with a tissue but asked for a rag and he insisted on cleaning it up for me."

"Thank you, Mr Greenhalgh. Now, go out there and win your tie. Good luck."

Yates and Barnes left the changing room and spoke briefly to Jack Davis who confirmed that, other than Elizabeth's car and the vehicle further up the road, he hadn't noticed anyone or anything significant when he'd walked the dog the Sunday morning of the tragedy. Leastways, not until he reached the car park on his way back where a number of members were standing chatting. Apart from James Winter no-one stood out in his memory.

For once even Sheenagh had nothing to say. The police officers drove back to the station to file reports before calling it a day. Two whole weeks had now passed and the Super was right. It was time they moved forward.

"We'll send Greg Thomas round to Greenhalgh's work place to see if anything else has struck his former business colleagues. Perhaps we've been concentrating too closely on Fisborough Golf Club and its members. Apart from his golf and bridge, which he played in the clubhouse or his own home, the victim doesn't appear to have had any other hobbies or interests. Except Babs Slater, of course. Even his card games were with his golfing cronies, none of whom have provided us with any useful facts."

Harry acquiesced, but, like Yates, he was still convinced the solution to the case lay at the golf club. Though he didn't rule out the person responsible could be associated with his personal life rather than his ability to play the game once described as 'a good walk spoiled'.

***

The following evening the garage confirmed that both Edward Greenhalgh and Dougie Watson filled up with Four Star petrol. The information was passed on to the police laboratory.

"We'll attempt to establish the grade and brand of the trace we're dealing with and get back to you. Is tomorrow soon enough? We've a heavy load on and a shortage of staff."

"I suppose tomorrow will have to do," Harry Barnes agreed and he imparted the news to DCI Yates.

"I guess one more day won't make much difference," Yates said.

"Greg Thomas has gone round to Hobson and Cartridge as you suggested."

"I don't hold up much hope of learning something we don't already know." The DCI sounded depressed. "Harry,

I can't see where we're going with this case and frankly I'm worried. I'm expected to get results."

"There has to be something we've missed. Something we just can't see. Shall we try another run through?"

"We could, but I think I've a better idea. When Greg gets back we'll call a meeting in the duty room of all officers who've been involved in the investigation. Try to get hold of those not on duty today. The promise of overtime might help but as you know resources are limited. It's just that one of them might throw a fresh light. The more heads getting together has got to be good. By the way, I looked through the emails WPC Fergus retrieved but nothing shouts out to me. They are the rantings of an angry old man but, surely, they don't present a motive for murder? The family are a better bet but it's finding the hard evidence that pinpoints who is responsible that's so difficult. Yet, call it a gut feeling if you like. I firmly believe we need to keep an open mind and, yes, I'm aware I keep repeating myself. There are a lot of people in the club and theoretically the murder could be down to anyone of them. It's like searching for the elusive needle in the haystack and getting nowhere."

"I disagree with you there, Raymond. I believe we have identified the leading players. Add a few extras and the culprit will come out of the pot."

"Let's hope you are right, Harry. Let's hope you're right."

PC Gregg Thomas returned and declared his visit had proved negative as nothing new had been disclosed. Carlton's business life was in exemplary order. The man hadn't put a foot out of place.

The meeting the DCI requested was set to go ahead mid-afternoon and everyone but DC Harper, who was on a day's outing, crammed into the duty room. Everyone consisted of seven police constables with DC Jacobs, Sergeant Barnes and the DCI himself making up the numbers.

Yates produced copies of notes showing all the information gathered on the main suspects and those on the periphery of the investigation.

"Information on these sheets may be new to most of you and I have pledged confidentiality to some of those concerned, until or unless it proves to have a bearing on the case. I'm trusting you to ensure that the information doesn't leave this room. We have reached the point when Sergeant Barnes and I, feel you should be made aware of the full facts as we know them."

He asked the officers to study the documents for a period before inviting them to make observations. At first there was silence. Officers exchanged glances.

"Come on," Yates ordered, "Let's hear from you?"

Again there was silence. Finally it was broken by Greg Thomas.

"You probably realise, Sir, we've discussed the case amongst ourselves. The consensus

of opinion is that one of the family or someone very close to the victim has to be responsible. Those blows to the head indicate a crime of passion and most of your listed suspects could be said to be passionately involved with Greenhalgh in one way or another. What I have just read adds to that view but it needs to be absorbed before I feel I can comment further."

DC Jacobs took over. "Take Babs Slater, for instance, she admits to meeting Greenhalgh just before he was killed. Now we learn she believed him to be the father of her son, who turns out to be Dougie Watson. It's pretty dramatic stuff. I have my doubts that Ms Slater could have committed such a frenzied attack, but if she acted, say, with

Dougie, then a strong case could be put forward."

"I still have doubts about his wife," another officer piped up. "Right from the start I felt she was capable of killing her husband. Now we are told she's tied up with his golfing partner, Grant Mason, that feeling has intensified. Both she and Carlton have brought out different emotions in people. He apparently thought a lot of himself and was open about his relationship with the Slater woman and Mrs G appears to be as cold as a block of Icelandic cod. My money's on her."

Soon most of the officers were exchanging views and the room was buzzing. Edward Greenhalgh came into the equation but, mainly due to the revelation in the DCI's documents, Dougie and Babs emerged as the most likely to be found guilty. WPC Pauline Fergus was the only one to emphasise that, on the evidence they had in front of them, no-one would be convicted. She also said it was important to look at the whole picture and not to jump to conclusions.

"Anyone on Detective Inspector Yates list could be the culprit, including the not so obvious names."

The meeting ended with coffee and tea all round and the funds even ran to some biscuits. Listening to what had been said left DCI Yates and Sergeant Barnes feeling refreshed even though the case hadn't been miraculously solved.

The DCI singled out Pauline Fergus for praise. "She's a very astute young woman," he observed. "Pity about that boy friend of hers. I might have plucked up courage to invite her out but, there again, she's far too young for me."

"You'd be surprised. Pauline's older than you probably think. She's twenty-eight."

"Really? I understood she joined the force straight from university."

"She did sort of, but that was after taking her Masters and a two year gap to travel the world."

"With those qualifications, how come she's started at the bottom of the ladder?"

"She could have applied to be fast-tracked, I guess, but I understand it was her idea to learn all the ropes from basics."

"That makes her even more interesting."

Harry was quite amused by Yates's remarks. "I thought you were opposed to relationships between officers?"

"I thought so, too. Let's get back to business. I'm glad we've brought the rest of the team fully up to date despite having to disclose some facts I'd like to have kept under wraps for the time being."

"We can trust our lot not to speak about what they know. They're well aware how gossip spreads and can hurt the innocent. Now, if it's okay with you I've a few loose ends to tie up regarding a couple more burglaries."

"Fine. I've to report the latest developments to Detective Superintendent Carter."

"Is there anything special scheduled for tomorrow?"

"Just more digging, Harry. No fireworks to let off, I'm afraid."

CHAPTER 12

Detective Chief Inspector Yates was wrong. The information he received early the next morning was explosive.

He was about to have breakfast when the phone rang. "Sergeant Barnes here, Sir. Think you'll want to join us. We're heading for Fisborough Golf Course. We have another body."

Within minutes the DCI was on his way. PC Thomas was waiting for him in the courtyard.

"Sergeant Barnes has gone ahead, Sir. The body is in the same area as before."

Thomas filled Yates in as they made their way towards the far end of the practice area.

"We received a call around seven-thirty from one of the grounds staff to say he'd been out cutting the greens for today's play. He switched the mower off to replace the flag at the fourteenth when he heard a dog barking. He's got a couple of terriers himself and recognised the animal was distressed. He thought it might be the dog that had been reported missing in the local paper. When he went to investigate, he saw a man lying in the rough with a light golf bag beside him. He knew immediately who the man was."

"And who was it?"

"Apparently it's one of the club's most senior members. Old Rob Stevens – in his mid-eighties. He thought he'd just heeled over and died until he saw the injuries to his head. Realising it was something even more serious, he called up the clubhouse but it hadn't opened, so he contacted the station."

By now they had reached Sergeant Barnes who was accompanied by DC Jacobs. The officers were in the process of sealing off the area. Callum Martin was standing inside his garden gate talking to a man Yates recognised as a reporter and the DCI also noted the large van pulling up at the front of Martin's house. Breakfast news had arrived with its ensemble of presenters and camera crew.

"Shit." Yates exclaimed angrily. "That stupid old devil must have contacted them."

"Yes," Barnes agreed. "More excitement to brighten up his day."

They followed the usual procedures and the course was declared closed for the day. Once the body had been examined in situ it was taken by ambulance to the morgue. The victim was estimated to have died the previous evening and must have lain out there in the rough all night.

Rob Stevens' body had been found before any players had ventured onto the fairways. A small group of regulars were gathered in the lounge by the time DCI Yates and Sergeant Barnes had left the crime scene in the safe hands of DC Jacobs and PC Thomas. A couple of constables had also been deployed to the usual search of the area. Fraser Turner, the grounds man who had found Rob Stevens, was still in a state of shock when the investigating officers entered. His hands shook as he sipped at a cup of hot sweet tea. The DCI asked if he felt able to tell them the events leading up to his discovery.

"I arrived on course around 6.45am and got out the grass cutter and began on the ninth green where I left off last night. As it happens I'd bumped into old Rob at the fourth yesterday evening. It was getting late and I warned him it would be too dark to play soon," he explained.

Rob Stevens had indicated he was only doing a few holes and was about to cut across to the thirteenth hole.

"His last words to me," the grounds man said, "were that he was getting too long in the tooth to play more than about five holes. The old fellow was laughing. I never caught sight of him again,"

"Did you see any other players on the course at the time?" the DCI asked.

"No, the fairways seemed to be deserted though it had been busy enough earlier."

Having nothing further to add, Turner poured another cup of tea from his pot.

DC Harper appeared and as it was obvious the old man's death was already common knowledge, he was ordered to speak to members to try to find out more about the victim whose age had been confirmed as eighty-five. He lived on his own in a small cottage in the village. Harper was informed that Rob's wife had died a few years previously and his only daughter was understood to live in North London with her husband. Harper was told to get in touch with the London force and arrange for them to notify her of the tragedy once her address was known.

Yates was relieved and grateful that the media hadn't released any details about the identity of the latest victim, hopefully because they didn't have any, unless Callum Martin somehow knew and had divulged them. Sheenagh was quick to inform the officers there had been a brief account of the incident on the eight o'clock news bulletin with a fuller report at eight-thirty but no name had been mentioned. Callum Martin was featured telling a presenter he had been awakened early by a dog barking. Looking out of his bedroom window he'd seen a small dog running up and down in an agitated manner beside what appeared to be someone lying in the rough close to where Carlton Greenhalgh's body had been found. He saw a grounds man arrive at the scene and the fellow pulled a mobile out of his pocket and within minutes the local police turned up. In view of the previous murder he felt it was his public duty to inform the media. According to Sheenagh and Jack he was wearing his best suit for the cameras and he expressed no sympathy for the victim and seemed even more pleased with himself than usual.

"Public duty, my foot," Harry Barnes said. "He wanted to get his nose in."

DCI Yates nodded. "I wonder if he's getting paid to give interviews."

"Probably trying to augment his pension."

"I guess you realise, Harry, this second murder could prove a godsend. Unless something turns up to indicate otherwise, it appears to point away from the Greenhalgh family."

"I guess so. Where does that leave us?"

The DCI regarded the question as rhetorical and began collating notes on the new case while Harry went off to join Harper in his quest for information.

"Found anything out?" he asked.

"Nothing really significant, Serg." Harper went over what he had elucidated.

He'd discovered that Stevens had given up playing competitive golf and was in the habit of going out alone to do half a dozen holes in the evenings two or three times a week. He was never around in the mornings and kept himself to himself for the most part although he joined in some of the social events. He was well liked by those who knew him.

When asked, Jack Davis said Rob was a nice old gentleman who'd been a reasonable player in his day. The majority of his friends were already dead but he enjoyed the odd game of bowls and was a member of the local bowling club. He also showed an interest in the village Historical Society.

"He was at their party here the other day. He sat next to Callum Martin and they found plenty to natter about, though I doubt if they were close friends." Sheenagh had come through to add to what Jack was saying.

Mr Winter left his office and joined them. "This is a disaster for the club. An absolute disaster. You can't help wondering if there's a serial killer at large and anyone could be the next victim. You officers have to pull your fingers out and get to the bottom of it quickly."

Harper and Barnes went through to Yates in the family room where he had once again taken over and closed the curtains.

"Mr Winter is right, of course," the DCI exclaimed when the club secretary's remarks were discussed. "We do have to come up with answers soon. Detective Superintendent Carter is furious a second murder has occurred under our vey noses."

"That's all very well," Harry fumed. "Why doesn't he come down here and sweat his brains out to solve the case. It's easy to sit behind a desk pointing the finger."

Yates looked daggers at his Sergeant who was quick to offer an apology. "Sorry, Sir, but this case has got me rattled."

He realised he'd been a trifle irreverent about his most senior officer and in front of a junior detective. Yates let it pass without comment, however, and they ordered tea and sandwiches from Agnes who looked close to tears.

"There's no rhyme or reason," she said. "Rob Stevens has been around for years, long before my day. He would never have harmed anyone." Sniffing into a tissue, she left the officers to their discussion.

"This latest crime is a real stinker," Harry acknowledged. "You felt there had to be something to explain Carlton Greenhalgh getting clobbered. But we'll be hard pressed to find a reason for Stevens' death."

The DCI looked serious. "I know, Harry, it's put a completely different slant on things. My main concern would be if both killings turned out to be random. Not that I believe that will be the case. There has to be a connection. The manner of the crime suggests that."

"You don't expect a place like Fisborough to be linked to murder, do you?" Harper said. "Did you notice the atmosphere in the dining lounge this morning? When Greenhalgh was killed it caused a buzz. Everyone was talking. But today there was a deathly silence. Maybe that's not the best choice of words. There was real fear. People are asking who's going to be next and they're running scared."

"Then it's up to us to find out who is responsible," Sergeant Barnes said. "At this stage we can't be positive the two deaths are down to the same killer. With both men being struck down with a golf club it's odds on they are. Different clubs but same method and same result." Yates pointed out.

"But should this prove to be the work of a random killer then the list of suspects is wide open. It could be anyone," Harper observed, dejectedly.

"That's one of the biggest worries we face but intuition tells me we'll find the answer close at hand. As I've said already, there has to be something that connects these crimes."

Agnes came in with the sandwiches and coffee. Though still obviously upset she had regained some of her composure.

"I expect you'd like us to close this room to members for another day or two while you conduct your enquiries?" she said.

"I've not decided what we want yet, Agnes, but it makes sense for today."

"I'll let Jack and Sheenagh know. They're really upset. They'd known Rob Stevens for years. It's like Sheenagh was saying through in the kitchen, he was such a harmless old man. Josie was beside herself and we've sent her home. Who on earth would want to take Rob's life? It must be the work of a mad man."

The officers tucked into tuna and mayonnaise and egg and cress with a relish that even murder hadn't diminished. They would need sustenance to keep up their strength to handle the investigation.

Barnes and Harper spent the afternoon gathering information from as many sources as possible as they strove to find the elusive, important, connection. DCI Yates revisited the scene of the second crime. He spoke to Greg Thomas who once again was placed in charge of organising the men conducting the search of the area. Unlike in the Greenhalgh case, there was no need to search for a weapon. The bloodstained seven iron used to strike Stevens had been left beside the victim's body and both were currently undergoing intense expert scrutiny by the forensics department.

"Not many metres from where Carlton Greenhalgh was discovered," Greg commented. "Maybe a bit closer to Martin's garden."

The DCI agreed. "The time factor is different, though. Stevens must have been killed shortly after the grounds man spoke to him at the fourth last night. Around eight pm as the light was fading. Apparently he was the only player still out on the course. The puzzle is what made him leave the fairway to go into this stretch of rough? We haven't found a stray ball."

Greg pondered for a few seconds before saying, "Maybe he heard or saw the stray dog. It ran off once the body was found but we caught up with it an hour later and it's the dog reported missing by Mrs Woodhams a few days back. It looked in good nick considering it had been on the loose for that length of time. Rusty, as he's called, has already been reunited with his owner."

"Wish we could bring him in as a witness," Yates laughed. "He'd be better than any other we have."

From their position, they noticed Callum Martin working in his garden. A television van still stood at the front of his house, but no crew was visible. Yates decided it might be a good time to have a word with Martin but he didn't fancy the job himself. Instead he delegated PC Thomas to the task and went over to the small, hastily erected, incident tent that was being used to house any objects of possible interest unearthed during the search of the rough. The WPC manning the tent informed him very little had been handed in.

"As you can see, Sir, it's just cigarette ends, tissues and an empty plastic bottle that once contained water. It was probably tossed into the rough some days ago. Nothing to get excited about, I'm afraid."

"Right, constable, I'm heading back to the clubhouse. Will you ask PC Thomas to join me in the family lounge when he returns, please? By the way, have you had tea or anything to eat?"

"Not since early morning, Sir,"

"Okay, I'll rustle up some lunch and have it sent out. How many of you are still prowling around?"

"Thank you very much, Sir. There are just the four of us, counting PC Thomas."

"That will be for three, then. Thomas can get something down at the clubhouse."

The WPC thanked him again and he left her sitting on a bench guarding the finds. Harper was about to go off duty when Yates walked into the dining lounge. DC Jacobs was already set to take his place.

"So, how did you get on?" the DCI addressed Harry Barnes and DC Harper.

"Not much to report, Sir. We had another word with the ground staff and according to them it was unusual for Stevens to play on a Tuesday evening. His normal days were Mondays, Wednesdays and Thursdays. Turner, the chap who found him, told us he'd said he was meeting up with a friend later. He assumed he meant after he'd gone home but maybe he was meeting whoever it was here," Sergeant Barnes said.

"That's possible. Did Agnes, Sheenagh or Jack report seeing anyone hanging around looking a bit lost last night?"

"Agnes had gone home by that time and the others don't recall seeing anybody other than Nick Baker and Brad Brown who dropped in for a quick pint. Jack is convinced Nick came on his own and that Brad joined him a bit later. He was sure they hadn't planned to meet. Neither appeared any different from usual and both were away before 7.30pm.

As no-one else came in Jack decided to close the clubhouse around 8.30pm because he was aware the course was deserted and he wanted to watch Big Brother on the television with Sheenagh in their private flat upstairs. Rob wasn't in the habit of coming in after he'd completed his few holes and they didn't expect last night to be any different.

"Okay if I go now, Sir?" Harper asked, and with the approval of his DCI he left.

"Did you find out who Stevens was friendly with at the club?" Yates asked Harry.

"We checked with Jack and Sheenagh and they said he was well liked but didn't have a particular buddy. That confirms what we were told earlier. How about you, Sir, did you come up with anything new? Did the rough yield any clues?"

"If you count an empty plastic water bottle, a few tissues and half a dozen fag ends as clues, then yes. We'll forward all the finds to the lab, of course, but don't expect miracles."

Both Barnes and Jacobs looked down. "Hey, cheer up," Yates encouraged. "We'll crack this, yet."

Harry put on a brave smile, "I'm sure we will but it's proving a tough nut."

PC Thomas came into the family room following his interview with Callum Martin. The DCI ordered lunch for those still out at the crime site as promised and ensured Thomas was fed before pressing him for a report.

"I don't know what to make of Callum Martin. He was co-operative and more than willing to tell me what he knew. He was in a hurry though because he'd been asked to put in another performance for the cameras and said he couldn't spare very long. He's recording a slot to be shown on the six o'clock news bulletin this evening." Greg Thomas finished his cup of coffee. "That was good thanks, Sir."

"So what did Martin have to say?"

"He was acting like he was some kind of celebrity. Absolutely loving the attention. He was so excited his hands were shaking and it wasn't through nerves."

Greg Thomas went on to repeat what Martin had told the presenter about being woken by the dog barking, opening his curtains to see what looked like a figure lying in the rough and a small dog frantically running up and down. The grounds man had approached and Martin said he saw him bend over the figure then take a mobile phone from his pocket. Martin claims he tried to contact us himself but couldn't get through. In a matter of minutes, uniformed police appeared and taped off the area.

"Had he heard anything unusual last night?"

"I asked him that and he said not. Then he threw me out to get ready for his next moment of stardom. He did say something a bit odd, though. He referred to the figure he'd seen as the old man and I wondered how he'd come to that conclusion. That information hadn't been released. He became a bit confused and said he'd just assumed it was because that's what it looked like."

"Interesting. Well, thanks for that, Thomas." I understand from Sergeant Barnes you should have knocked off along with DC Harper. Thanks for staying on."

"That's all right, Sir. I can carry on if you like?"

"No, Constable, you've done enough for now. We're about to return to the station ourselves. It will be another busy day tomorrow, no doubt. I'd like you and DC Harper to come straight here in the morning and continue to dig for any connection between the two victims. You'll probably draw a blank but keep trying. All those involved in the Greenhalgh investigation will need to be questioned about this latest death."

Greg Thomas left and the DCI asked Jacobs to remain at the clubhouse and to keep his eyes and ears open. Sergeant Barnes fixed up an overnight presence at the scene of crime. A couple of the investigation team would be spending the long dark hours in the small tent with only a wooden bench to relax on.

Together the DCI and his Sergeant drove back to Fisborough police station to make out their reports. Rob Stevens's sixty-three year old daughter, Emily Marsden, had arrived from London and was, not surprisingly, in a very distressed state.

"My father was a good man, hard-working and honest. I'd begged him to come and stay with Joe, my husband, and me but he couldn't bring himself to leave the village. I thought he was safe here. It's such a quiet, pleasant place. Who in their right mind would kill an old man? The manner of his death is incomprehensible."

DCI Yates nodded in agreement and both he and Harry extended their sincere sympathy.

"Joe is disabled, you know, and we have no family. I can only stay the one night, I'm afraid. I'll be leaving first thing in the morning."

The officers promised to keep her informed of developments. "We are doing our utmost to solve this case quickly," Yates stressed as he shook her hand. The utter despair of relatives in these situations never failed to move him.

Detective Superintendent Carter had left a message indicating he was waiting impatiently at headquarters. It was nearing midnight when Yates lifted his brief case and headed home. His answer machine was flashing on the hallway table. He pressed the button to listen to the recording.

"Hello Darling, Mother speaking. Hope you are all organised for a week on Saturday. I sent out the invites on your behalf a few days ago but it's still open to you to extend the list and add some more work colleagues. Karen phoned me to say she'd been trying to reach you to explain she can't make it because she's going to be in Paris. She wants you to give her a ring."

"Oh shit," Raymond Yates exclaimed, using his favoured expletive. He'd forgotten to phone Karen as promised. His mother must have sent her an invite. In truth, he'd forgotten about his forthcoming birthday party. Work had been all absorbing and there was still a chance he'd have to miss his own celebrations. Not that it would worry him, personally, but he was aware his mother had put in a lot of effort and she would be affronted. He checked his watch. There was nothing for it. It was too late now. He'd have to sort things out in the morning.

CHAPTER 13

Raymond Yates phoned Karen first thing in the morning.

"Sorry to ring so early but I reckoned this was my only chance to catch you."

"And I'm sorry I had to turn down your mother's invitation to attend your party. I'll be in gay Paris."

"So she told me. Who or what's sending you over there?"

"Not work. I'm going with a colleague, Mark Johnston. We're kind of seeing each other. Sorry to drop this on you but it's been a while since you and I got together and Mark came into the picture. We've a lot in common."

Yates felt himself getting a bit hot under the collar. Karen was dumping him. He could hardly blame her. He hadn't exactly been paying her much attention lately, but after all the time they'd known each other he guessed he'd taken it for granted they'd end up together.

"Are you okay?" Karen asked.

"I guess so. This is a bit of shock though. I thought..."

Karen interrupted, "I'd hoped we'd meet up and I could let you know face to face, but you're so elusive. Do you ever check your messages?"

"Not often enough it seems. Not on my home phone.

You'll be aware I've been busy work-wise?"

"I read the papers and you've featured. We'd never have worked out. I need someone who has got time to spare, occasionally. The clock's ticking and I'd like to have children before it's too late. Didn't see that happening with you, Raymond. Sorry,"

Karen rang off and Yates was left to consider the consequences. He didn't blame her. He wasn't sure how he felt. His mother would come out with. 'I told you so'.

He'd been very fond of Karen, but that was it. Would they eventually have drifted into marriage? He didn't know the answer but something told him the break was probably for the best. He could play the field again with a clear conscience, if he could ever find the time. One day, no doubt, he'd settle down.

He picked up his paper and read the headlines. The Fisborough Golf Club murders had been relegated to page five and once again Callum Martin was quoted. He read what the man had to say this time and it was nothing new. He moaned about the disruption to village life and his in particular and said he hoped there'd be no need for more deaths.

That, the DCI thought was an odd way of expressing it, but then Martin was a bit of an odd ball the way he propelled himself to the front of the media reports whether it was in the papers or on the television. He'd come across his kind before, a pensioner brightening up his dull life. Such people usually got in the way of their real inquiries.

At the station he joined Harry Barnes and they resumed the task of collating the evidence they had managed to put together. The time of death was confirmed at between seven-thirty and ten pm and death was definitely caused by a blow to the head. The number seven golf club was confirmed as the instrument employed. Nothing else significant came out of the Lab report, not even a fingerprint to point them towards the perpetrator.

A fragile link between Bradley Brown and Rob Stevens had been established by DC Jacobs. Brad's father was once employed by the same timber company as Stevens and there'd been animosity when the latter, who had been in a senior position with the firm, had accused Mr Brown senior of mishandling a consignment of timber. Brad's father lost his job but always maintained he had done nothing wrong. The rumour at the time indicated that he had procured some of the consignment for his own use. The company hadn't considered the matter important enough to report to the police and had dealt with it privately. However, ill-feeling had persisted between the two families for a time.

Edward Greenhalgh was said to have been seen arguing with Rob Stevens recently when the old man had cut in front of him and his partner as they played a tie one evening. Edward Greenhalgh accused the old man of interfering with their game and hadn't minced his words.

"I wouldn't think there was much in either incident. Bradley's link is historic and Edward's just part of golf's trivial ramifications. But I will ask Jacobs to delve a little just in case something comes out of either report."

"Yes, but I suspect we'll be wasting his time. Anything else?"

"WPC Pauline Fergus came to speak to me. Says she's been watching Martin's appearances on the telly. She's concerned he's enjoying being in the limelight a little too much."

"That's pretty obvious to everyone."

"Apparently she's studying in her spare time for a qualification in criminal psychology. She's been analysing

Martin's behaviour and is worried the man has a problem."

"I'd agree there all right. The guy's proving a bloody nuisance but if PC Fergus thinks there's more in it I'll need convincing. Tell her I would like to speak to her in your room this afternoon if she's free. Around 3.30pm would suit me. I've decided to pay our friend Martin a personal visit right now. Want to join me?"

"Give me five minutes to tie a few things up and I'll accept your offer."

"See you in the car park in five minutes, then. Do you have your car here?"

"Yes."

"Then you're driving."

DCI Yates was leaning against the car park wall when Sergeant Barnes joined him.

"That was precisely seven minutes and thirty seconds, you're late."

"My fault, I needed a pee."

"In which case you're forgiven," The DCI laughed.

"Thanks for that. Does Callum Martin know we're calling on him?"

"I thought we would surprise him. Hopefully he's at home."

"Is this visit based on WPC Fergus's comments?"

"Actually, no, though I found them interesting. She's a very bright young woman, however, I had already decided to let Mr Martin have some of the attention he craves and I'd like to take a peek out of his bedroom window."

Harry Barnes gave his senior officer a quizzical look.

"Just keep your eyes on the road, Sergeant." Yates quipped.

There was no sign of Mr Martin working in his garden

but the front door was opened before they reached for the bell.

"I'm on my way out," Callum Martin said as they approached. "I want to catch the post."

The letter in his hand was already stamped and the DCI recalled passing a letter box just a few metres down the street.

"If I remember correctly the next collection's at 2 pm and the box is almost on your door step. We can wait while you nip along to it or you can leave your letter posting till we've finished speaking to you," Yates said.

"I've got a third option. I speak to you and then you can drop the letter in the box for me after," Martin said, a big toothy grin transforming his formerly sombre expression.

"Done," said Yates. "Now, are you going to invite us in?"

They were shown into a compact lounge. The furniture was heavy and a little too large but the décor was fresh and light. A pile of cuttings taken from the newspapers was strewn across a low table.

"Nice room," Harry said as if he meant it. His past experience of interviewing people in their homes told him it was always useful to pay tribute to the premises.

"You should have seen it before I took over. Falling to pieces the place was. It had lain empty for over five years. Needed gutted but I saw its potential. One of which was being so close to the golf course." Martin gestured towards the lounge window. "Fat lot of use that's turned out to be."

"We've heard about your struggle for membership. Maybe the death of two members has improved your chances?"

A glimmer of a smile lit Martin's face but it was soon removed. "I'd like to have a look out of your bedroom window," the DCI added.

Yates was already heading for the stairs with Sergeant Barnes on his heels. Callum Martin huffed up behind them.

"So run through what you saw when you opened the curtains yesterday morning."

"I was lying in bed and woke up when I heard the dog. I could tell from its bark something was up."

"Used to dogs then are you Mr Martin?" Sergeant Barnes asked.

"I haven't got one here yet. Nervous it might escape and play havoc with the greens, but I've lived with dogs most my life. Love the creatures. They don't bite as much as human beings."

"Tell us again what you saw when you looked out?" The DCI encouraged, sensing Martin was gearing up for another performance.

"I was a bit bleary eyed having just woken up but apart from the dog pacing up and down and straining his lungs to be heard, I made out a figure lying on the grass over there." He pointed to a spot in the rough. "I was still staring out when the grounds man came along on his machine."

"So how did you react?"

"Well, I'd have phoned you lot but the other guy had reached for his mobile and by the time I'd gone for the phone it was engaged and I guessed it was him on the line to you."

"I believe in your statement to PC Thomas you said you saw the figure of an old man. What made you think it was an old man?"

"I dunno. The other officer asked me that. I think it was the way he was lying."

"You could tell it was a male figure?"

"I believed it was."

"But you didn't know?"

"Of course not. How could I?"

"How indeed?" the Detective Chief Inspector commented. "But you are aware of the identity of the victim now?"

"Of course. The whole of the village knows."

"Did you know Rob Stevens well?"

"Not very. I'd met him once or twice."

"And where was that?"

"I'd seen him at the Historic Society a few times. He knew quite a lot about the old village."

"And elsewhere?"

"I'd seen him around sometimes."

"We've been told you sat next to him at a recent party the Historic Society held."

"That's right I did. It was just the other day."

"What did you talk about?"

"I don't remember. It was just general talk. Where's all this questioning going?"

"We're trying to get a clear picture of Rob Stevens, Mr Martin. Did he tell you anything about his life? His friends for instance?"

"He told me he lived on his own and he had a daughter who stayed somewhere in the north of London. I gathered he didn't see much of her and he didn't appear to have any close friends. At least he didn't say he had."

"So you got the impression he was a bit of a loner?"

"You could say that. He played golf on his own."

"How did you know that?"

"I think he must have told me. Anyway, it was in the paper wasn't it? He was on his own when he was clobbered."

"Apart from his killer or killers, yes. Are you sure you

didn't see anyone the night before he was found?"

"No, I'd have closed the curtains by then."

"When was that?"

"Around a quarter to eight I'd say."

"And you heard nothing after that?"

"The telly would be on. I'd have been watching."

"Watching what?"

"Can't remember. Whatever was on."

"Shall we go back downstairs?"

They made their way down to the sitting room.

"Now, I'd like you to cast your mind back to the day of Carlton Greenhalgh's death. You reported that you'd witnessed what appeared to be an argument between the victim and a lady with blonde curly hair."

"That Babs Slater. I didn't know who she was at the time but I've seen pictures since and it was her all right, I swear."

"You don't have to. Ms Slater has admitted meeting with Greenhalgh and having a disagreement with him."

"That proves I was right then. Nothing wrong with my eyes."

"Glad to hear it. So maybe you can tell us more about the person you thought you saw further down the course that day in the rough?"

"I only had a sort of vision of someone."

"Man or woman?"

"I'm not sure. I'd guess it was a man. I think a woman would have stood out."

"So this person, was he wearing a black top, blue trousers and a white visor?"

"That's right blue trousers."

"Thanks, Mr Martin"

"By the way, I don't suppose you saw the six iron lying beside Mr Stevens' body."

"It was a seven iron."

"Are you sure? Have I made a mistake?"

"I'm quite sure. I saw it. A seven iron."

"You do have good eyes. Thanks for your help. We may need to speak to you again. Just routine, of course."

"Of course, that's fine. Glad to have helped. Oh, don't forget my letter. You said you'd post it."

"So I did." DCI Yates took the letter and the two officers left, leaving Callum Martin feeling even more like a celebrity.

"I had a suspicion about Martin and reckoned if I questioned him for long enough he'd slip up. Seven iron, indeed. To know that he'd have to have been told or been up close. From that window even my eyes couldn't have picked out the club was a seven iron."

"Are you going to bring him in, Sir?"

"I'll see if he can hang himself a bit more first. He went along with my description of the person he said he'd seen in the rough and I made that up. We'll keep a discreet watch on the fellow in case he has a notion to wipe out any more Fisborough golfers."

"You really do believe he's responsible?" Sergeant Barnes couldn't keep the doubt from his voice.

"Responsible? I'm not certain but I'm as sure as I can be the guy's involved in some way. And to think he was throwing himself at us and I dismissed him. Maybe I could have saved Stevens if I'd cottoned on to Martin sooner."

"I don't think any of us suspected him, Sir, except perhaps WPC Fergus. Are you positive we shouldn't bring him in now?"

"Yes. We haven't got enough evidence. But I want that man kept on twenty four hour surveillance. I've an idea that

I'm going to try to put in force which could give us what we need."

"Going to let me in on it?"

"Not yet. I've a few things to arrange first. Drive me back to the station and keep this morning's activities under wraps. I'll let you say your piece when the time comes. Meanwhile you've a report to draw up even if you can't make it common knowledge."

"Yes, Sir, my lips are sealed."

"Fine. Forget the station we haven't eaten yet. Let's drop in for one of Sheenagh's tasty dishes."

"Good idea, but we'd better put that letter in the post box first."

CHAPTER 14

"Glad you came in," Agnes said. "A lot's been happening here. But I think Sheenagh wants to tell you. I know my place," she laughed.

The Detective Chief Inspector and his Sergeant were intrigued and hadn't long to wait as, within minutes of their arrival, Sheenagh bustled through to the dining lounge eager to impart her news.

"You'll never know what went on last night," she began.

"No, but I reckon we soon will. Go on, then, Sheenagh, spill the beans."

"Well, we'd quite a busy evening. Babs Slater came in and she joined Dougie Watson at his table. Shortly after Bradley Brown put in an appearance and he went over to their table and sat down. They ordered drinks and were deep in conversation for some time. Then Bradley told everyone he wanted to make an announcement. He said the time was right. Then he told us Dougie was Babs Slater's son and that he was his father. You could have knocked us down with a feather." Sheenagh's face was glowing as if she had imparted some huge news. She was surprised when neither the DCI nor his Sergeant reacted. "You already knew didn't you?" she accused.

"Yes but we promised to keep it quiet until they were ready to speak out."

"Babs says she is glad it's in the open and Dougie looked a bit sheepish at first but seemed happy enough. Bradley, however, was like a school kid who'd just won the top prize. He was so excited. Jack gave them a bottle of champagne to celebrate their coming out, as he called it. Babs stressed that she and Bradley were just good friends. It was a bit of a shock but after all the bad news it was good to hear something quite nice, and who knows what the future might hold?"

Agnes came in with their soup and toasties and Sheenagh asked how the investigation was going.

"We're making progress," he said.

"Glad to hear it. Everyone's been really jittery since Rob Stevens' death. It will be good when we can put it all behind us."

"Let's hope that's soon," Harry Barnes said. "We'd better eat before it gets cold."

"Heavens," the DCI looked at the big clock above the bar. "Is that the time?"

"A few minutes fast, I think, but it is nearly 2pm."

"I've that meeting with WPC Fergus at 3.30pm and loads to do before then. Hurry up and finish. We need to get back to the station."

The DCI was confident the Fisborough Golf Club cases would soon be concluded and he said as much in a phone call to Detective Superintendent Carter, who expressed his relief. "I've received an invite to your big birthday party, by the way. Brenda and I will be delighted to come along. I'll be dropping a note to your mother."

The Super and his wife hadn't figured on Yates' own list of guests. His presence would mean he'd have to be on his best behaviour. It might put some of the team off drinking to excess as well. He bet his mother had thought of that when issuing the invite. She hated the loss of dignity that often resulted from over indulgence and would be mortified if the party ended in a brawl.

WPC Pauline Fergus rapped on the door promptly at three-thirty. Sergeant Barnes had indicated he was tied up but hoped to join them later. The DCI felt slightly awkward about facing the woman police constable. He could not deny his attraction towards her but he knew he had to bury it, at least for the time being. With Karen out of the picture who knew what might develop?

"Come in and take a seat. Sergeant Barnes informs me you have expressed views on the Golf Club murders and I'd be interested to hear them."

Pauline sat down and composed herself. Clearing her throat, she embarked on an account of her studies in criminal psychology and explained she'd taken a keen interest in the media broadcasts relating to the case. She had, she said, paid particularly attention to the interviews involving Callum Martin.

"I'm convinced Mr Martin is suffering from a form of paranoia concerning his unsuccessful bid to join the golf club."

"He certainly goes on enough about it. But how do you think that relates to the murders?"

"I don't know if it does. It strikes me that he has developed a need to keep himself in the limelight. He's revelling in the role he's playing. The question I've been asking myself is, does his interest stem from an involvement in the actual crimes? The guilty usually act in one of two ways. Either they sink into the background and try to hide, or they push themselves to the fore often trying too hard to convince the viewer or listener that they sympathise with the victim, when all the time they are simply seeking to be the centre of attention."

"I wouldn't describe Martin as sympathetic and what about motive? Would someone like Martin kill purely to secure attention?" Yates asked.

"There have been such cases reported as you must be aware. I get the impression Mr Martin has got caught up in a situation and can't escape even if he wants to, and, incidentally, I don't think he does want to. He's actually enjoying himself and it's given him a stage on which to voice his grievances. He's convinced he's been harshly treated. It's like a bee in his bonnet that keeps on buzzing. He thinks about it when he wakes in the morning and those thoughts are still there when he goes to sleep at night. He probably dreams about it. He can think of little else. In other words he is obsessed and obsession can be very dangerous in certain people."

The DCI was listening intently. Pauline had a lovely speaking voice and a way with words that forced you to listen, but had she said anything he hadn't already considered himself?

"Carry on," he encouraged when she paused to gauge his reaction. "Am I to understand you think Callum Martin is our murderer?"

"I'm not sure of that, but I'm convinced he is involved in some way. That is, if he didn't commit the crimes, he may well know who did and for some reason he's not coming to us with that information. You can dismiss this as pure speculation but I base my opinion from observation of his actions. It's as if he is following a pattern. He may have drawn that pattern up or someone else might have drawn it up for him. I don't know but I do have a strong feeling there could be more victims if we don't get to the bottom of the case soon."

"Are you convinced both cases are definitely connected?"

"Yes, Sir, I'm certain of it."

"Thank you, Pauline, before I learned from Sergeant Barnes that you had expressed certain concerns, I had already decided to pay a call on Martin this morning because I, too, had been concerned at his craving for the limelight in a case he had at first glance been drawn into as a casual witness. Initially in the Carlton Greenhalgh case we sought him out, he didn't come running to us but he then seized the opportunity to publicise his moans. I had him down as a silly old man who was making a bit of a nuisance of himself at first. But his persistence in gaining attention finally made me look at him more closely and, like you, I began to wonder and questioned if he was involved in the killings."

"Did you learn anything new from this morning's visit, Sir?"

"Enough for me to put him under surveillance. I'm not prepared to go into detail but he did lie to me today. I have to gather more evidence before detaining him. I may bring him in here next time we need to talk but I'd like to give him more rope to either hang himself or prove me wrong. This course of study you've been following, do you intend to become a criminal psychologist?"

"It's too early to say, Sir, but I do find the study absorbing."

"There have been several occasions when I've been impressed with your work. Not just the work, the way you conduct yourself in general. I think you could go far in the force."

"Thank you, Sir."

"It's been a pleasure."

PC Fergus left with a spring in her step. She had impressed a man she respected. DCI Yates was someone to look up to and besides that she really liked him.

The Detective Chief Inspector's gaze remained on the WPC until the door closed behind her. He told himself again that he'd have to be careful. He found Pauline Fergus intelligent and attractive. A dangerous combination, especially when he remembered what Harry Barnes had said about her boyfriend.

Hardly had the door closed on his interview with Fergus than Sergeant Barnes arrived. "I see I'm too late," he said. "How did it go?"

"Very well. She expressed herself clearly and affirmed several of my own views which was interesting."

"So, what now?"

"I have placed Martin under surveillance. DC Harper and DC Jacobs, together with your PC Thomas, have been delegated to the job and will work three hour shifts. Thomas has shown he could make a useful addition to the headquarters force. I like what I've seen."

"He's been with us for about nine months, Sir. Came straight from college where he specialised in Art and IT. Not especially relevant subjects."

"Art requires strong powers of observation and IT skills are the bees knees these days."

"I guess you're right."

"I suppose we should question Bradley Brown about his old man's involvement with Rob Stevens. See if he had any hang ups about the fellow. And then there's Edward Greenhalgh. We'd better find out how deeply his rows with Rob went or if they just had nuisance value. Can a couple of your officers handle it? We're pushed for man-power due to the surveillance."

"Are the team working all night?"

"That's what I've arranged. I know you'll be asking why. Call it instinct if you like. I believe Martin is involved in the murders in some way and if he isn't the perpetrator there's a chance he's in danger. I'm just following my gut. Anyway it will be good experience for them, especially young Greg Thomas."

"Okay, I'll see what I can arrange. The WPCs could be given a chance to cover the Greenhalgh and Brown follow ups."

"Good idea. I don't want either guy to think we regard this as a big thing, though everything is in handling these crimes. I'm proposing to hang on here a bit tonight in case something develops from the surveillance job. How about you?"

"If you don't mind, Sir, I'll head home when I'm finished. I promised Mary I'd take her to the school tonight. They're holding one of those parents' evenings. She likes us both to go along."

"Fair enough. I'll catch up with you tomorrow."

Sergeant Barnes left Yates in his office and made for the duty room to compile a list of the next day's proposed activities. There were a couple of small time incidents to investigate in addition to assigning two constables to the interviews with Bradley Brown and Edward Greenhalgh.

He decided to leave thirty minutes early and drop in at the golf club on his way home.

He found Dougie in the Professional shop with Graham and noted that Bradley and Edward were scheduled to play next day. Although at different times, both were down to play in the morning. Maybe the WPCs could catch them before or after their games for a chat. They could sniff around for any other news at the same time and they'd be putting in one of those important shows of presence as the DCI referred to their visits.

Sheenagh, Agnes and Josie had nothing to impart and Jack was at an hospital appointment. James Winter acknowledged Harry with a brief wave as he was leaving for home and the sergeant spotted Nick Baker and Grant Mason coming off the eighteenth green. Harry wondered how so many golfers managed to get time from their work to indulge in their favourite sport. As he drove away he caught sight of Elizabeth Greenhalgh's blue BMW approaching the car park. It had been some days since she had come under scrutiny. The trouble with golf clubs was they had far too big a membership.

As usual dinner was ready and waiting on his return home. The family of four sat down to macaroni and cheese garnished with sliced hard boiled eggs and tomatoes. A plate of garlic bread on the side completed the main course. Homemade treacle pudding and custard followed. When he had finished eating Harry, somewhat reluctantly, got ready to go with Mary to the school. His son's were fairly academic and reports were always promising but, in keeping with most of their friends, their hearts were into sport. It was the same when he was a boy. Some things never changed, though he was concerned computer games were becoming more time consuming.

CHAPTER 15

PC Greg Thomas agreed to be the first to take on a shift to watch Callum Martin's house for action of any shape or form. With Harper and Jacobs, he had conducted a survey of the exterior of the house and its surroundings. They selected an observation site on the road opposite the dwelling, where the slope of the land afforded a clear view of the front entrance to the premises, although the rear garden view was somewhat restricted. It was essential to observe without being observed and they were lucky that Martin's house occupied an isolated position, with the golf course to the rear of the property and a small woodland area facing it across a rarely used lane. The neighbouring houses were detached and had large private gardens affording a high degree of privacy.

The woodland offered them the concealed vantage point they needed. But it would be eerie out there through the night and Greg was glad his first stint of duty was during the daylight hours. Sergeant Barnes had suggested they take a low stool with them so that they could give their legs a rest from time to time and they had enough cover to be able to move around without attracting attention. Ideally they would work in pairs, but man-power was limited and, important as the Fisborough case was, it wasn't the only investigation taking place.

Although they couldn't dismiss the idea Martin might leave his home via the back door and trespass straight on to the course as they understood he had done previously, they were confident the front entrance would be favoured at night. Callum Martin didn't own a car, a fact that initially they felt eliminated the need for a police vehicle, marked or otherwise, to be in the vicinity. On reflection, however, they decided it made sense to have a car within easy reach to cover the possibility of Martin being picked up by someone.

Greg had been instructed to leave his uniform in the locker and wear casuals and, having ascertained that Martin was at home, he took up his position at 2.30pm. His orders were to follow Callum Martin if he left the house. Greg's excitement at being given such an assignment dulled as absolutely nothing happened for the first two hours of his three hour shift. He had just sat down on the stool for a minute when Martin's front door opened and the old man walked down the garden path. He was carrying his stick. Carrying being the operative word as its tip rarely touched the pavement. Greg waited a few seconds then emerged from the trees and began walking along the pavement opposite the elderly man. He watched from a distance as Callum Martin walked to the Main Street and went into the post office. The village store came next. He emerged with a bag of shopping, turned and retraced his steps home.

PC Greg Thomas resumed his vigilance from the woodland. Unless Martin had spoken to someone in the Post Office or the store he had made contact with no-one. Greg wondered if he should have followed the man into both premises. Had he in fact slipped up? He was new to this kind of policing and felt slightly unsure. He was relieved when DC Harper appeared. Greg hadn't recognised him at first. He was dressed in jogging bottoms and a sweater and had a baseball cap drawn low over his head. A pair of sunglasses hid his eyes.

"Any chance of a light mate?" he asked as he pulled up beside Greg.

"Don't smoke," came the reply.

"Neither do I," Harper laughed, pushing back the cap and removing the glasses to reveal himself.

"Like your gear. I'll try to do better tomorrow," Thomas said, looking down at his blue shirt and grey slacks.

"You're fine as you are. It's essential we look different. That way he hopefully won't realise we're keeping an eye on him."

"Do you know what all this mystery is about?" Greg asked.

"Not exactly, but I can guess. The old chap must have aroused suspicion in some way. Either he is in danger or he is considered to be a danger. It's important we report everything. Where he goes, who he meets, that kind of thing."

Greg felt a bit guilty about not following Martin into the shops. He hadn't even watched him through the windows. Needless to say he didn't confess his failings to DC Harper.

The men bade each other farewell and Greg walked some distance through the wooded area prior to breaking cover and heading back to the station to report to Sergeant Barnes before going home, knowing he'd have to be back for another shift around midnight.

DC Harper had taken up his post just after half-past-five and was due to finish at eight-thirty. Unlike Greg, he was called into action within the hour as Martin headed out for the second time that day. This trip took him to the community hall. Harper phoned the station to ask what was on.

"It's a meeting of the Historic Society, starts at seven and finishes about nine."

"Is Sergeant Barnes in the station?"

"No but DCI Yates is."

Harper asked to be put through to the senior officer.

"Do I go inside, Sir?"

"Yes, what are you wearing?"

Harper told him. "I've a change of trousers in my hold all and my sweater is reversible. I could add a moustache and metal framed specs."

"No need to overdo it, but try to stay incognito. Hopefully no-one will recognise you. You don't live locally."

D C Harper entered the hall and, having been welcomed and asked for a two pound entrance fee, took a seat a little behind Mr Martin. A

speaker was giving a talk about the village at the time of the First World War.

Harper found it interesting and welcomed the fact that he was sitting comfortably indoors and not standing around among the trees.

He observed Martin nod to the people in adjacent seats but he didn't enter into conversation with them. When the meeting finished Martin was among the first to leave. DC Jacobs was already waiting outside the building and he signalled to Harper as he left that he would take over.

Callum Martin went straight home and was observed to pick up the phone in his lounge before closing the curtains. Within a short period of time the lounge light was extinguished and the house was in darkness. Assuming the old man had gone to bed, Jacobs risked going across the road. He looked round the rear of the house and saw the back bedroom curtains were drawn but a faint light shone through them. Jacobs knew this was Callum Martin's bedroom because in his testimony he said he had looked out of his bedroom window and seen the figure of Rob Stevens lying on the golf course.

Jacobs crossed back over to the trees and settled on the stool to have the supper he'd brought with him. Every so often he took a stroll through the woodland but kept the entrance to the house in view the whole time. When Greg Thomas arrived at eleven-forty-five pm, he was more than ready to go home but he lingered on to chat to the young constable.

"Is this the first time you've done this kind of job?"

"Yes," Greg confided.

"I thought so. You'll probably find it a struggle to keep alert through the night. Chances are nothing will happen during your shift. The old boy hasn't stirred since quarter-past-ten. Must be sleeping soundly. No-one has approached his house. In fact no-one's even walked down this lane. The temptation is to sit for too long but it's not a good idea. You need to keep moving or do a few exercises. I play games. Give myself some mental arithmetic. Like guessing what time it is. It's never as late as you think. There's the name game, too. Go through the alphabet thinking of names of boys beginning with each letter, then do the same with girls. It's a kid's game really but it keeps you awake. You reckon you'll be all right?"

"Sure of it. Thanks for the advice though. I've brought my music and the earphones."

"I wouldn't admit that to Sergeant Barnes in the morning. Don't let it distract you from keeping your eyes focused on Martin's house and I'd limit the use of those headphones.

On this job you may need all your senses. I'll be on my way then. See you sometime tomorrow."

Greg settled down to his watch. Everywhere was so dark. The trees rustled in a slight breeze, and he imagined he heard a fox. Switching on his IPod, he shut out the sounds of the night and it helped relax him. Mindful of DC Jacobs's warning he turned the music off at frequent intervals and admitted the IPod might not have been such a good idea. He noted Callum Martin's lane had just one lamp at the end of it. The half moon and a few stars provided the only other glimmer of light. He sat on the stool and was on the verge of falling asleep, when he nearly fell off and was jerked into wakefulness.

Thankfully, the house across the road remained dark and silent. The whole exercise seemed a waste of time. He got up and walked up and down flapping his arms against his sides to keep warm. He was well wrapped up but he sensed a chill in the air. DC Harper arrived to relieve him a little after 2.30pm and whispered a greeting. It seemed odd to be speaking in whispers. There was no-one about to hear them speaking yet it seemed appropriate.

"Okay son, you can get to bed now. I assume there's been no movement"

"Deadly quiet," he said, then felt himself shudder at his choice of adjective.

"You get accustomed to it," Harper said. "I've been doing this kind of thing for six years. Mind you, not in the countryside. I'm based at headquarters and used to plenty going on even in the middle of the night, and it's well lit, too. Good in some ways but more difficult for you to disappear into the surroundings. I like bus stops, actually. You can hang around them even after the last bus has gone without attracting attention and most provide shelter from rain and a bench to sit on even if it is cold metal and does your arse no favours."

Greg left Harper to his shift and the latter settled into a routine of pacing up and down as he watched not only the house, but the sky changing mood. Clouds were gathering to blot out the stars and hide the moon, by morning he was sure it would be raining. It was at times like this he wished he still smoked but it would be frowned upon. Even the glow from a fag could give you away when you were doing surveillance work. His three hours dragged. DC Jacobs took over at five-thirty am and two hours later a light came on in the downstairs lounge of Callum Martin's house. Morning had broken and with it a steady drizzle had started to fall.

A milk wagon trundled noisily along the rough surface of the lane and two cartons of milk were left on Callum Martin's door step. Seconds later, DC Harper got his first glimpse of Martin as he lifted the milk and disappeared indoors again. He had been in view long enough for the DC to note he was fully dressed and looking spritely. The sound of whistling heralded the arrival of a paper boy. It was the normal start of a normal day's activity.

Greg arrived in jeans and casual rain jacket to take over from Jacobs for another stretch. He'd grabbed a few hours sleep and was feeling refreshed. Jacobs was preparing to head home when they were alerted by the sound and sight of a car pulling up outside Callum Martin's house. A young dark haired man, smartly dressed in a suit, stepped from the vehicle.

"Bloody Hell! Do you see who that is?" DC Jacobs exclaimed.

Greg Thomas nodded. "What's he doing here?"

The two officers watched as Edward Greenhalgh walked

up Martin's garden path and rang the door bell. Callum Martin answered and gestured to Greenhalgh to go inside but the later remained on the doorstep as they engaged in what appeared to be an animated conversation.

"Wish we could hear what they are saying" Greg said.

"The way Greenhalgh is gesticulating it's serious talk, but I can't begin to guess what it's about," Jacobs said, shaking his head. "Lip reading's not one of my many skills."

"Nor mine. What do we do now?" Greg asked.

"You mean what do *you* do now? It's your shout, man, I'm off duty as from four minutes ago. If you need advice phone the station. Maybe the DCI or Sergeant Barnes have clocked in. "

"But…" began Greg.

"Look, ring and let them know. Keep up your observation. I parked my car in Hill Street. If I scoot I can reach it before Greenhalgh leaves and try to keep tabs on where he goes next."

Greg Thomas stayed under cover and observed Martin close his door as Edward Greenhalgh returned to his car and drove off. Jacobs reached his vehicle in time to settle into position some distance behind Greenhalgh's Audi.

Greenhalgh rounded the corner and turned first right into the entrance to Fisborough Golf Club.

A call to the station informed him that Greenhalgh was scheduled to play at ten o'clock and a WPC was already at the club hoping to have a chat with him before he went out on the course. The station confirmed they had received a call from PC Thomas about Edward's early visit to Martin and she'd been briefed to question him about it.

Jacob's was happy the force was on the ball. Greenhalgh would be surprised they were aware of his movements and would be off guard.

Meanwhile, Greg Thomas settled down on the stool to eat the bacon sandwich his mother had made him for breakfast and swigged it down with a can of coca cola.

Back at the station the DCI was busy following up the idea he'd had the previous day.

A call to the nearest television studio in Larkfield, about an hour's drive from Fisborough village, was fruitful. Sean McArthur, the producer and presenter of 'Matters of the Moment' agreed to the request he put to him.

"It will mean postponing an interview with a council official about the benefits of recycling, but that shouldn't be a problem. What you have proposed is potentially a much more exciting topic for the programme and it could go out on my seven-thirty slot this evening. Could you drop in and discuss exactly how you'd like it to be conducted. Do you think the old boy will play ball?"

"He'll be over the moon. There's nothing he likes better than a bit of publicity. If you could ring him personally to invite him to the studios he won't be able to resist. Could you send transport to pick him up and maybe suggest a drink before and after the programme? I reckon my budget will run to the transport and Callum Martin will lap it up."

"Okay I'll put on my most persuasive voice and see what I can arrange. We cover expenses incurred by our guests and pay them a fee, so forget about your budget. Can you give me his details?"

The DCI provided Sean McArthur with the contact information for Martin and set about preparing some notes on what he hoped the broadcast would achieve. Having convinced himself Martin was concealing something he had a feeling Sean McArthur was the man who could trick the pensioner into revealing what. He'd already arranged for their psychologist, Vera Clarke, to be on standby to watch the broadcast and report her observations. DCI Yates admitted there was a chance he was mistaken about Martin and it could be a costly waste of time. He was prepared to risk being left with a red face – it wouldn't be the first time.

Sergeant Barnes came into the office having dealt with some general matters that had arisen.

"Good morning, Sir. I assume you received the message from PC Thomas?"

"Yes, I found it most interesting and maybe it proves my intuition to keep an eye on Martin was justified. I wonder what instigated Greenhalgh's visit? That young man deserves some serious consideration. I was about to try to find you to suggest we nip down to the Golf Course right now. There's still forty-five minutes until his tee off time and according to Jacobs he's already down at the club. Jacobs has gone off duty but your WPCs are already having a chat with him, and I'd like to hear Edward's version personally. Are you free?"

"I can be. Everything's set up here."

"Good let's get on our way, then."

Once again the DCI allowed Barnes to act as chauffeur.

"I've to drive to the Larkfield Television Studio, shortly." He told Sergeant Barnes of his plans. "Sean McArthur has been very co-operative. Let's hope Martin falls for the bait."

"Don't think there's much chance he'll turn down the offer of appearing on the telly again, especially if a tempting pay packet is dangled before his eyes."

***

"I'm expecting Sean McArthur to ring my mobile any time after ten-thirty. We'd better pray Martin hasn't another engagement. I can't wait to see our star performer in action."

When the two officers walked into the dining lounge at

Fisborough Golf Club, Edward Greenhalgh was looking annoyed as he sat at a table with the police women.

He stood up when Yates and Barnes approached.

"This is harassment. I've told your constables everything and now I'll have to get ready for my match. Not that I'll be in the right frame of mind, thanks to you lot."

He began to walk away from the table but the DCI restrained him. "Wait a minute or two longer, while I check your explanation for calling at Callum Martin's house earlier this morning. Can I see your notes, Constable Wallace?" The WPC handed over her notepad. "Thank you."

Yates studied the words written on the pad. "So you went to apologise?"

"Yes, my mother had witnessed one of our spats on course and made me. Said it didn't look good seeing she was to be Lady Captain next season. Her exact words were "it wasn't gentlemanly," and she's a stickler for good behaviour on the course."

Yates couldn't restrain a smile. "Very commendable. Do you always do what mummy asks?"

"Of course, not. But in this instance...." Edward Greenhalgh left his sentence unfinished.

"Okay you can go now but we may need to speak to you again."

Greenhalgh left, his face red with anger and discomfort.

"Good shot," Yates acknowledged as minutes later he and Barnes witnessed Edward Greenhalgh on the first tee.

"Yes, no sign of his game being affected," commented Sergeant Barnes.

"I wonder if he's a fan of the Sean McArhur show? Talking of which," the DCI said, "It's about time I heard from the studio."

No sooner had he stepped into Sergeant Barnes car to

return to the station than his mobile phone rang. It was all arranged. Callum Martin would be picked up and taken to the television studio mid-afternoon and would be briefed for his evening appearance, which would follow a sumptuous dinner and enough wine to loosen his tongue.

"As if it needs loosening," Harry Barnes laughed when his superior officer passed on the details of the call.

"Do you want me to go with you?" he asked.

"Not this time, Harry. I'd like you and Mary to have a nice, quiet night in front of the television set. I'll be looking for a review in the morning."

CHAPTER 16

"It's nice to see you again."

Sean McArthur greeted Detective Chief Inspector Yates with a firm handshake and ushered him into a reception room.

"Thank you for taking my idea on board," Yates said. He wasn't always grateful to the media. On several occasions it had interfered with an investigation he'd been conducting and he'd cursed it. There were other times when it had been a help and he hoped this one would fit into that category.

"Go ahead and fill me in," McArthur said.

"You'll appreciate I can't tell you the full details of our investigation. Callum Martin has come to the fore by his own efforts. I regarded him as a rather annoying fellow who was always trying to hog the limelight until quite recently. Now, one or two small things have forced me to give him closer attention."

"So do you think he may have committed the Fisborough murders?"

"It's possible. I do have a gut feeling the man is involved in the crimes, yes."

"I take it you're under the impression both deaths are connected?"

"No doubt about that in my mind but there's still a possibility we have more than one perpetrator. I take it you've read the press reports on the cases and watched your own channel's coverage?"

"Of course, it's not every day we have crimes like this almost on our doorstep and I have to confess a personal interest. My son is a member of Fisborough Golf Club. He's a former junior champion – Richard McArthur. He only manages a few games a year these days as he's away at Leeds University. He knew Carlton Greenhalgh and his family, but didn't have much contact with them. But I digress from the business in front of us. How would you like me to approach the interview with Martin?"

"I thought it would be a good idea to let him express his grievances with the club first before coming to the questions I'd like you to put to him. Once he's got his moans off his chest he'll hopefully be more relaxed. I've made some notes for you and outlined what I'm hoping we achieve. I've set up a criminal psychologist to analyse what he says and how he reacts. Personally, I think the man is pretty gullible."

"That should help. I'd be grateful if you could run through your notes with me in case I need anything clarified. Let's get a drink."

"You can have what you like but I'm here in an official capacity and being on duty I'll have nothing stronger than a black coffee."

"Coffee it is, then."

Detective Chief Inspector Yates and Sean McArthur put their heads together and came up with a satisfactory approach to the programme.

"I think I'm going to enjoy tonight. A prod here and there and the guy should open up. Most people do."

"I've seen your broadcasts and I'm confident if there's

something to be dragged out of Callum Martin you'll get it," the DCI said.

"Are you going to stay at the studios to watch? I would offer you dinner but I guess you don't want to disclose you're behind this and even though I love my food, I couldn't manage two meals in one evening. I've already arranged to eat with Martin. I usually dine with my guests. It helps put them at ease for what's to follow."

"I'm tempted, but, unfortunately, I've to get back to the station but I'll be in touch later. Thank you again for your co-operation."

"It's a pleasure. I remember the last time you and I got together when you were dealing with that series of armed robberies. Must be at least two years ago."

"That's about right. We had a successful conclusion in that case, so here's hoping. We haven't had a lot of clues thrown in our direction in this investigation. There are too many possible suspects."

DCI Yates left the studio's and headed back towards Fisborough Station. On the way a taxi passed in the opposite direction and Yates had an uncanny feeling he knew the passenger.

WPC Wallace and her colleague Amanda Church had placed a report on their interview with Bradley Brown on Harry's desk. He had, they said appeared surprised when they'd raised the issue of his father's connection with Rob Stevens. "Never given it a thought," he'd told the officers. Bradley went on to say he didn't believe his late father had held a grudge for long. He certainly never mentioned it, though at the time he had been very upset by the accusation, but he found other employment and moved on. The constables had formed the impression Bradley Brown was speaking the truth.

Yates went in search of Sergeant Barnes and found him in the canteen.

"I felt like a cup of tea before knocking off, Raymond. Sorry, I didn't know you were back."

"You don't need to explain yourself to me, Harry. You more than cover your hours."

"Do you want to join me?" Harry asked.

"Not this time. I'm going home to prepare for tonight's entertainment. You should leave soon, too."

"How did you get on with Sean McArthur?"

"Surprisingly well. I actually quite like the guy. He's very professional and was quick to cotton on to what I want out of this interview. I'm optimistic we might learn something. Heaven knows we need a breakthrough. I read the report on the Bradley Brown interview. It sounded pretty straightforward. I've a feeling we can cross Brown off our suspects list."

"I'm happy about that. For someone with the reputation of being a joker he's looked downright miserable since he discovered Carlton's body. That is until he found out he was Dougie's father. Now you can't wipe the grin from his face and even Babs has cheered up. I wonder if those two will get it together again one day."

"You've been reading too many fairy tales, Harry."

"That'll be right with a couple of growing lads in the house. All they're interested in is computer games and football."

"I could think of a lot worse. What's happened to your Constable Pauline Fergus? I haven't seen her around today."

"She took some leave that was overdue, but she'll be back in the morning."

"Good. I'd hoped to catch her. Any chance you could let

her know about Callum Martin's starring role. It was after she'd given me her view on the man that I got the idea to give him the limelight on McArthur's show."

"I'll try to get in touch. She wouldn't want to miss it."

The DCI left Barnes to finish his tea and made for home. He stopped at the Chinese take away for a carry out. Quick meals were becoming a habit. He'd have to get down to some healthy living. He might even fit in that game of golf before long.

The roads were busy and Yates got held up at every traffic light. His emergency blue light lay on the back seat of the car but he resisted the temptation to stick it to the roof and make his journey easier.

He warmed his sweet and sour chicken in the microwave for a few seconds and poured a glass of red wine. A fine Rioja he'd brought back from Spain on his last holiday. Its rich velvet taste soothed more than his throat and if it had not been for the Sean McArthur show, he might well have fallen asleep. He turned on the television to catch the end of a soap and waited impatiently for 'Matters of the Moment' to begin. The familiar face of the presenter came on to the screen to announce a change of guest.

"Tonight, replacing a programme on the benefits of recycling, we are taking a look at the disturbing crimes that have occurred at Fisborough Golf Club recently. Members are facing up to not one, but two, murders on their course. It has been a very distressing time for everybody concerned. My guest tonight is Callum Martin whose house backs on to the Fisborough course. Mr Martin has featured in a number of our news reports on the crimes and he has a story to tell us that deserves to be heard."

The cameras turned to introduce Martin. He was wearing his suit and his white shirt was complemented by a light blue and navy striped tie. The make-up department had done a good job. Callum Martin looked younger than his seventy-three years. He fidgeted for a few minutes in his seat before settling into his usual tirade about his failure to gain membership to the club despite all his efforts. Sean let him have full reign and the elderly man took advantage of it.

"It's disgraceful the way that club operates," he said. "It's like a closed shop. I've practically lived in its grounds for the past two years but still I haven't been granted access."

"Is that because the club's membership list is full?"

"That's what they say. Apparently I don't have any priority. Well it's not full now, is it? What with the two deaths, there has to be two vacant places at least."

Sean McArthur nodded, "So potentially, from your point of view, some good might come from these crimes? I believe you actually witnessed them?"

"Well not actually witnessed them, but I was able to give the police officers some important evidence. Not that they've done much with it as far as I can see."

Callum Martin went on to describe the argument he'd seen between Carlton Greenhalgh and Babs Slater, though, he pointed out, he hadn't known who it was at the time. He went on to describe the man he'd seen in the rough at the bottom of the practice area, wearing a dark coloured top, a white visor and blue trousers.

Watching on his home television, Raymond Yates shook his head. This was the figure he, Yates, had described using his imagination. The old man had simply cottoned on to it. Unless he'd convinced himself the person existed.

"And did you see this figure before or after the body had been found?" McArthur asked.

"It was before. I didn't see anyone after except the police

when they came round to interview me and I told them about the argument and the other person in the rough."

"You were working in your garden at the time, I understand. You were able to see all this from it?

"Didn't I just say so?"

"But you didn't hear anyone cry out?"

"No I was mowing my lawn. Never heard a thing."

"Let's move on to the second murder," Sean said. "What happened then?"

"I was in my bed and I became aware of a dog barking. It belonged to Mrs Woodhams and had been missing, you know, and she was in a rare state about it. The darn dog made such a racket I got up and opened my curtains to see what was up with it. There it was, pacing up and down frantic like and behind it I saw a figure lying in the long grass just metres from my back gate. I assumed something pretty serious had happened and then the green keeper drove up on his grass cutting machine."

"And what did you do, Callum?"

"I was about to phone the police station when the green keeper got out his mobile and I left it to him."

"What did you think had happened?"

"It was near to where the last crime was committed and I realised they'd found another body."

Callum Martin continued with his story. He was becoming more animated all the time. His hands were constantly waving about and his face was alight with excitement. DCI Yates feared for the old man's blood pressure. Sean McArthur was nodding appropriately and encouraging Martin to keep talking.

"You must have been extremely alarmed by what you saw?"

Callum Martin paused for a few seconds before

answering. "I guess I was more curious than frightened. I wanted to know what was going on."

"Did you go outside to investigate?"

"No. I decided to leave it to the police. They were swarming the place within minutes. I watched from my window. The figure was lying there and there was a seven iron golf club nearby. They picked it up and put it in one of those plastic bags they use."

"A seven iron? You're confident of that?"

"Yes, I could tell from my window. I know my clubs. It was a seven all right."

"You must have remarkable eyesight for a man of your age, or were you wearing glasses?"

"I don't own any glasses except for drinking my nightcap. I like a whisky before I go to bed." Callum was laughing at his own joke and looked pleased with himself.

DCI Yates knew no reports had been made public detailing what club was used to kill Rob Stevens. Having stood and looked out of Martin's bedroom window, he knew, too, that it would have been impossible to determine the number of that club lying beside the body. Yates had already surmised Martin could only have known this if he had been there and witnessed its use, seen it close up at some time or been informed by someone who had. It was their most important piece of evidence to date and now the old man had repeated it on national television. The programme moved into its last ten minutes. Yates had hoped for more. He needed more.

"Well, I have to admit you're a very brave man, Callum. I admire you for coming forward and telling us your story. Do you think Fisborough Golf Course will come up with any more murders?"

"That depends, I suppose."

"Depends on what Callum?"

"If the killer decides to knock anyone else off."

"So you believe we may be dealing with a serial killer or killers?"

"I wouldn't go so far as that. But you never know."

"How do you think these incidents might affect your application for membership. I assume you still want to be considered, despite what has happened?"

"Of course, I do. There has to be vacancies, now. They can't pull that one, can they?"

"I suppose not, but I've been given to understand there is a waiting list."

"That's what they say. But I'm right up there now, Mr Greenhalgh told me."

Yates jumped from his seat. Was he about to hear what he'd been waiting for throughout the interview? He sat down again and tried to remain calm as he watched and listened. Sean McArthur was doing a great job.

"Mr Greenhalgh, that will be Edward, the son of the first victim?"

"That's right but he's nothing like his father. He's got much more sense. He understands the point I've been making about priority. He's backing me to the hilt and he has influence. His mother has influence, too, and she understands where I'm coming from. He's promised me I shouldn't have to wait long to become a member. And not before time."

"Well, that's very encouraging. Is there anything else you'd like to say, Callum, before we wind down?"

"Just thanks to you for giving me the opportunity to speak out."

"That's it for this evening folks. Join us on Thursday when we'll be bringing another matter of current interest to your screens."

Yates reached for his remote and silenced the television. He needed silence to absorb what the programme had thrown up. So Edward Greenhalgh and Callum Martin were in cahoots in some way. They'd appreciated there had to be a connection between the two men following Greenhalgh's early morning visit. Things were starting to come together but the ultimate solution had yet to be revealed. Greenhalgh and Martin were an unlikely combination and where did the former's mother fit in?

The phone rang and Harry Barnes was curious to know what the DCI had made of the programme.

"It was an interesting broadcast and well worthwhile. Callum got a little carried away at times and that played into our hands. I've a growing feeling the man may have placed himself in the limelight once too often"

"I agree. He could be in danger."

"That's what I'm thinking. Could you have a couple of officers standing by to watch him on his return."

"You want to bring him in?"

"I'm not sure but I'll let you know after I've spoken to our psychologist. I might want him to bring someone out."

"Okay I'll put Thomas and Harper on surveillance again. Together this time. I called them off for the duration of the broadcast. They should both be at the station at the moment."

"You do that. But I want another couple of officers watching the rear of the house and someone's got to tail Edward Greenhalgh. I'm going to beg the Super' to allocate us a few more men from headquarters. I'll keep you informed. I'm on my way to the station now."

"So am I. I'll see you there."

As soon as Sergeant Barnes rang off the criminal

psychologist was on to Yates.

"I'll give you a full report when I've compiled it but I reckon Martin's being taken for a ride. The likeliest assumption is he knows something and this fellow Greenhalgh is promising him all sorts to keep quiet. Unfortunately bringing Greenhalgh's name into the conversation with Sean McArthur might have triggered something we don't want. The old man could be in danger. I'd be very careful if I were you, unless you want more bloodshed."

"I don't want that even though I find Martin a pain. I'll take care. Thanks Vera."

Again the phone was red hot. This time it was Sean McArthur.

"Hi there, Raymond. Did I give you what you wanted?"

"You were exceptional. Handled things expertly, as I knew you would."

"He was a bit of an oddball to deal with. Absolutely convinced of his rights but he did open up, didn't he?"

"Yes, our only fear is he could have opened up a bit too much for his own good."

"Yes, I wondered about that. I'll need to dash. We're about to eat."

"Enjoy your meal. We'll be keeping close tabs on him and on a certain Edward Greenhalgh, don't worry."

CHAPTER 17

Detective Chief Inspector Yates arrived at Fisborough Station within minutes of Sergeant Barnes and they met up in the latter's office. Sean McArthur had explained Callum Martin had elected to dine immediately after the show rather than before and had been treated to drinks and light tit-bits prior to his appearance. Allowing about an hour for the meal, he calculated his guest would be on his way home around 9.30pm and providing the traffic was within reason he should be back by, or before, ten-twenty.

They had no way of knowing if Edward Greenhalgh had caught the broadcast but someone, perhaps Elizabeth, was bound to tell him about it. In that case he was likely to be furious his name had cropped up, and an angry Edward Greenhalgh wasn't a pleasant thought. Would he re-act as soon as Martin returned or wait until the morning? He would possibly already be panicking especially after his early call on Martin had been monitored and commented on. As it stood they still had very little on the guy. Certainly not enough evidence to pull him in.

Yates and Barnes went back and looked at the file on Carlton Greenhalgh's murder. Edward was adjudged to have had the time and opportunity to kill his father. It was common knowledge the two men hadn't got on. Edward was educated but very much a mummy's boy, which contrasted with the tough, arrogant character he chose to portray. But lots of criminals adored their mothers. Had he hated his father enough to have swung that club and hit him? And how did Martin fit in? Was it possible he had seen more than he has admitted? Did Edward have some sort of control over the old man or was it vice versa? Was Martin actually blackmailing Edward into helping him join the golf club? There were still a lot of questions awaiting answers.

After much discussion the officers decided that, if nothing occurred overnight, they would bring Martin in and apply some pressure in the morning to see if they could make him talk. Martin wasn't an unintelligent man. In fact many might regard him as quite a wise old owl but at his age he was vulnerable and if the prize were big enough, gullible.

Having checked their surveillance team was set up, they were both preparing to leave when WPC Fergus came in.

"That was a most uncomfortable viewing. I felt quite sorry for Callum Martin. He walked into a few leading questions. I guess you set it up, Sir?" she said.

DCI Yates nodded. "I know where you're coming from, Constable, but in this job you have to do things you don't always approve of. According to Sean McArthur, Martin actually enjoyed his evening. We gave him a chance to have his say and he gave us some useful information, and, by golly, we needed that. This case has been treading water for too long. Now, it's beginning to move and move fast. Are you questioning my judgement?"

"No, Sir, of course not, but my recent training tells me you might have exposed the old man to danger."

"We are well aware of that and have his back covered. Is that all you wanted, Constable?"

WPC Pauline Fergus was blushing as she left the room.

She was aware she'd trodden on her Chief's toes and it had hurt her more than him.

"You were a bit tough on the girl, Raymond," Harry said.

"Maybe that's because she's right," Yates conceded. "Look, Harry, it's been a long day. I suggest you and I get some shut eye and review developments tomorrow morning."

Sergeant Barnes followed DCI Yates out of the building and into the car park. It had indeed been a long, busy day.

Back in his home, Yates put some music on then having looked up Pauline Fergus's number, lifted the phone and dialled. "Sorry if I came over a bit harsh but you were voicing my own fears."

"Thank you for phoning, Sir. I was speaking out of order, but you did ask me to watch the programme."

"At this time of night on your private line I'm Raymond and you're Pauline. I was wondering if you would like to come to my birthday party next Saturday night? I've already invited most of the team and those not on duty appear to be coming but you weren't around. You can bring your boyfriend if you like."

"If you mean Ryan, I've finished with him. Would it be okay to come without a partner?"

"Of course. I'll give you one of my mother's little cards tomorrow. It's got all the details on it."

So, Raymond Yates thought, if I make a move I'm not walking into a heavy tackle. She's free, I'm free, who knows?"

With this happy thought Yates went to bed and fell asleep more easily than he'd expected.

His good mood was still apparent next morning, there having been no calls during the night. He grabbed a quick breakfast of cereal and toast and left for Fisborough Police

Station where he found a message awaiting from Detective Superintendent Carter to call him when he came in.

"Shit," he said to himself. He'd been so wrapped up with everything last night he'd omitted to get in touch with his superior. He hadn't even warned him about the broadcast.

The Detective Superintendent was calmer than Yates expected. "I'm sorry I didn't fill you in, Sir. It was a particularly exhausting and busy day," the latter said.

"So I gathered. I only caught the end of McArthur's programme but guessed you'd been involved. Did you get what you wanted from it?"

"We did and so far there have been no adverse repercussions. I've set up a surveillance on both Edward Greenhalgh and Callum Martin. There's been no movement through the night. I'm considering bringing Martin and Greenhalgh in for a grilling shortly. Separately, of course."

"Keep me informed and good luck."

Detective Superintendant Carter had let him off the hook lightly. Yates knew he'd broken protocol.

He sought Pauline Fergus out and handed her an official invite.

"You don't need to contact my mother. If you can attend I'll pass on the message."

"Thank you, Sir. I'm free that night. I'll look forward to it."

Before Yates had the chance to continue chatting up the WPC, the phone on reception rang.

"It's Greg Thomas, Sir. He says it's urgent."

Yates checked his watch. It was eight forty-three.

"There's been a development, Sir. Edward Greenhalgh's mother has just arrived at Martin's house. She's about to ring his bell. Do we intercept?"

Elizabeth Greenhalgh? Yates had expected her son,

Edward, to contact Martin.

"See what happens when he answers the door and stand by to pounce. Don't switch off. I want a running commentary. Is DC Harper with you?"

"Yes, Sir. He's breaking cover a bit further up the road and intends to cross over to Martin's place if need be."

"Good thinking. Chances are she won't try anything, though you never know. Is she driving or on foot?"

"There's no sign of her car, Sir,"

"Is the back of the house still covered?"

"Yes, Sir. DC Harper speaking. I've alerted them." The link had become three way.

DCI Yates caught Sergeant Barnes as he came in and passed on the latest news.

Barnes picked up a connected phone and the two officers listened to the start of Constable Greg Thomas's commentary.

"You'd better take a patrol car and get down there quickly, Harry," the DCI ordered. "They might need assistance."

"That's the door opening now, Sir. Mrs Greenhalgh and Martin are talking and neither looks very happy. DC Harper's on their side of the lane and is approaching slowly. They aren't paying him any attention. Hold on a minute, Elizabeth Greenhalgh has just shoved the old man inside. The door's ajar still but they're out of sight."

"Right, Harper, I want you to try to reach Martin's door without being seen to assess the situation. I appreciate you won't be able to contact me in case they hear you so act on your own initiative."

"Will do, Sir."

Swiftly but stealthily DC Harper followed instructions and within seconds was crouching outside the open door.

He could hear raised voices from inside.

"You stupid man, what possessed you to take part in that show? Drawing attention to yourself and bringing in my son's name."

"I wanted people to know he was on my side. I wasn't saying anything about seeing you that morning or about the night Rob Stevens was killed. I keep my promises."

"You'll be very lucky if Edward keeps his. He missed the programme last night but I didn't and I've told him what went on. He's furious with you and you know what he's capable of if he's angry."

"I didn't think....."

"That's obvious. You didn't think. You do understand you're involved in this up to your neck. Utter one word to anyone and your chances of joining the club are zero? Maybe I need to make you understand."

There were sounds of a scuffle and the old man cried out.

DC Harper stepped away from the door and signalled to Constable Thomas to join him.

"We're going inside now, Sir," he whispered. "I've heard enough. Will we take them both into custody, Sir?"

The DCI assented and the two police officers entered the house. Elizabeth Greenhalgh was standing over Callum Martin as he cowered against his lounge wall. His left eye was reddening, as if it had been at the end of a fist. She had lost it and kept raging over how stupid the man was.

The pair looked astonished when Harper and Thomas burst in on them.

"We've been instructed to bring you both in to Fisborough Police Station. Detective Chief Inspector Yates wants to talk to you." Harper said taking a hold of Mrs Greenhalgh's arm.

"Don't touch me," she yelled. "This is monstrous. An

assault on human rights,"

"You can tell that to my superior, Madam," Harper replied, gripping her arm even firmer.

Callum Martin had slumped to the floor and Constable Thomas assisted him to his feet.

"Come on Granddad. We're going walkies."

A screech of brakes outside announced the arrival of Sergeant Barnes and two squad cars. "Okay boys?" he asked.

"Absolutely, Sir."

"Let's get them into the cars."

Callum Martin accompanied PC Thomas in one patrol car, whilst Elizabeth Greenhalgh travelled alongside Sergeant Barnes and DC Harper and protested all the way to the station. "I've an appointment at ten and an important meeting this afternoon."

"I don't doubt it Mrs Greenhalgh. With your solicitor, I expect," Sergeant Barnes quipped.

Back at the Station, Pauline Fergus and Greg Thomas were dispatched to collect Edward Greenhalgh from his office while Harper filled in a report of what he and Thomas had overheard at Martin's house.

"We need to take all three of them to headquarters," Yates said. "There's not enough room in this station, Sergeant. Fix things up and join me there."

The three suspects were taken in a convoy of separate cars to Laureston Police Headquarters. Elizabeth and Edward were both still hotly protesting but Callum Martin was unusually subdued.

Martin was shown into interview room one while the mother and son were left to cool down in rooms two and three respectively.

Sergeant Barnes drove up shortly after the main party

and, having gone over all the morning's revelations, with his senior officer he sat in as the DCI interviewed Callum Martin. The latter was bowed over a desk, his head supported by his hands. He looked up as the officers entered the room.

"I should have known it was all too good to be true," he muttered.

"Would you like to tell us what was too good, Mr Martin? You may make a voluntary statement if you wish but I have to warn you it could be used in evidence later. Would you prefer to have a solicitor present? You may well need one at some point."

"I haven't done anything wrong. It's them you should be talking too. They're the guilty ones, so I don't need any lawyer."

"Let's hear your story, then? Sergeant Barnes will be recording what you tell us. That will help when we prepare a statement for you to sign, okay?"

Martin nodded.

"Right, start with the day of Carlton Greenhalgh's murder."

"I was in the garden working, see, when I saw a man and woman having an argument on the practice area." Martin began to relate his account of that morning. The DCI listened for any diversion from his previous statements. " It was Babs Slater, though I didn't know that was her name at the time. She moved off in the direction of the clubhouse and he carried on walking up the hill for a bit. It was then I realised it was Carlton Greenhalgh."

"So when Babs Slater left him, Carlton was fine?"

"I don't know about fine, but he was alive. I heard a voice call out to him and seconds later his wife stepped out from the trees."

Yates and Barnes exchanged glances as Martin continued. "I knew her slightly. Everyone said she was a bit of a tartar, like, and my was she storming into him. Telling him off something awful. As he turned away, she snatched the golf club he had in his hand and swiped him with it. He fell to the ground. She dropped the club beside him and hurried off down through the trees towards the car park. I was rooted to the spot for a few minutes then thought I'd better go and take a look to see if he was okay. I'd made for the gate rather than jump the fence because my legs were a bit wobbly and I'd only taken a few steps when I saw young Edward running up the practice area to where his father lay in the rough. He didn't spot me so I went back into my garden. When I turned round Edward had picked up the club and was bringing it down on his father's head. Carlton didn't cry out or make any sound at all. I reckoned he was dead."

"And you are absolutely certain you saw both Elizabeth and Edward Greenhalgh strike Carlton with the club?"

"Of course I am or I wouldn't be saying so. I was shocked and wanted to keep out of it so I got the mower going. When I looked up again Edward was carrying the club as he made off, but then he stopped, wiped it, and went across and flung it in the ditch."

Callum Martin paused in his narrative. "Can I have a glass of water?"

DCI Yates turned to the constable standing by the door and told him to fetch the water for Martin. The elderly man looked exhausted and DCI Yates asked him if he was able to continue.

"Yes. Now I've started I want to get it all off my chest. Where had I got to?"

"Edward flung the club in the ditch."

"That's right. He was wearing his golf glove. I got the impression he'd been playing. He went on down the practice area to the end nearest the car park. When I took my eyes off him a few minutes later, a player was coming along searching the rough as if he'd lost his ball. He rushed over to Carlton, took one look, dropped his bag of clubs and went off down the fairway as if he was being chased by a ghost."

"Did you recognise the player?"

"It was Bradley Brown. I carried on till I'd finished the grass and went round the front. I'd to sit down for a while because I felt bad. I knew the other guy had gone for help and I just wanted to stay out of it. When your constable came I didn't tell him all I'd seen."

"Why was that?"

"I don't know. I was scared, but later that evening I began to think and thought maybe I could get something out of it. Not money, but perhaps I could improve my chances of getting into the club if I had the right people on my side. I contacted Edward and told him what I'd seen and promised I wouldn't say a word if he and his mother agreed to back my membership application. I said I'd hated Carlton as much as they had. Edward told me his father had treated his mother badly and was making her life a misery with his affairs and he had threatened to cut Edward out of his will because of all their arguing. He said they hadn't planned to kill Carlton. His mother was angry and humiliated by his behaviour that day and impulsively struck out."

Martin went on to tell the detectives that Edward told him he'd met his mother as she left the practice area and she'd claimed to have hit Carlton in a fit of temper. Edward explained he'd gone to see what state his father was in and found him lying there suffering terribly.

"He said he'd hit him again to put him out of his misery like you do with an injured animal. He told me it was an act of mercy."

Detective Chief Inspector Yates listened intently without interrupting , but at this point he decided to pose a question.

"Didn't you think you might be exposing yourself to danger by telling Edward what you'd seen?"

"Of course, I'd figured that out. I'm not as daft as some folk think. I'd written it all down and sent it to my lawyer for safe keeping. It's in an envelope marked to be opened if anything happens to me. I let Edward know what I'd done. It was a kind of insurance. Edward and I got on well when we chatted and he agreed I should have priority seeing I'd bought my house so close to the course. He also said that Carlton's death left a vacancy on the waiting list which could be in my favour. He said I should be grateful to him and his mother for that, and I was. I could see what he was getting at. He went on to say that there were a few people holding down membership places who shouldn't be and that he'd had a run in with old Rob Stevens, who was a menace because he could only manage a few holes and kept cutting in and interfering with games. He said it was a pity we couldn't get rid of him, too, and make another space. As his mother had no connection to Rob, if he were to be killed it would be like a diversion. Make the police have to consider other things such as there being a serial killer striking at random."

"What did you think of that idea? Didn't you point out that would be wrong?"

"I suppose I should have. At first I assumed he was joking. But when I thought about it, I could see the sense of it and realised he was serious. He said if I could arrange for Rob to come to my house after golf one evening he could put his plan into action. I was a bit shocked at first but then I sat next to Rob at the Historic Society dinner and he moaned all the time about his arthritis getting worse and how he never had any visitors and was lonely. He said sometimes he felt life wasn't worth living and he wasn't looking forward to another birthday. I got the impression he'd be happy to die."

"Did you arrange to meet Stevens again?"

"I remembered what Edward had said and invited him over on the Tuesday evening. He said it wasn't one of his playing days but he'd make an exception, play a few holes first and then join me. I suggested he came in the back way straight from the course. After that he seemed to cheer up. I let Edward know he was coming, so I suppose I set him up. It seemed quite exciting at the time like something in the films. Rob never turned up at my place and I guessed Edward might have dealt with him. The suspense of not being sure was huge, so after a while I slipped out just to check, like. He was lying there with the seven iron at his side. It made my stomach turn and I went back in and had a dram, hoping it would help me sleep, but I couldn't settle and only dozed. So, you see, I wasn't surprised at what I saw in the morning. Though I hadn't counted on that dog causing such a racket."

"Well, that clarifies how you knew the weapon was a seven iron. And I believe it was you who called in the media?"

"I could speak out because I'd had nothing to do with his death, really. I got a bit carried away, being in the papers and on the telly. It was exciting. Made me feel important, like. Edward didn't seem to object to any of it at first but then he came round yesterday morning and said I was to calm down and stop drawing attention to myself but I got the invite to appear on Sean McArthur's 'Matters of the Moment' and I was offered a huge fee. It would pay the central heating for the whole year and I was feeling a bit hard up, so I accepted. After all I still had my insurance didn't I? I knew Edward wouldn't be pleased but I wanted the money and I hadn't meant to mention his name, it just came out. I thought it made him sound quite good, actually, but that mother of his was like a dragon this morning. She really frightened the wits out of me and she punched me one. I was glad when your men turned up. Heaven knows what she might have done. Now I've told you everything can I go home?"

"You do realise, Mr Martin, what you have told us places you in a very difficult position? You have admitted that you perverted the course of justice in the case of the murder of Carlton Greenhalgh by not disclosing the truth. In your own words you confess you set up Rob Stevens. Admittedly, I think you were under the influence of Edward Greenhalgh and his mother, but you were aware you were putting Stevens in danger when you told Edward about his plan to visit you. I'm afraid we have no alternative but to charge you with conspiracy to murder in the second case and withholding evidence in the first. You will be remanded in custody and I'd advise you to contact your lawyer. The fact that you have given us such a full account of what happened could be used in your plea for a degree of leniency, but these are extremely serious charges. Is there a family member I can contact?"

"No, I was divorced years ago and she died of cancer recently. I've a son somewhere in the world but he lives abroad and there's been no contact with him since he was a kid."

"We will assist you with notifying your lawyer then you

will be taken to the remand cell. Thank you for your co-operation."

"You can't keep me here. Who's going to cancel my papers and the milk?"

"List your concerns and I'll have someone make sure they are taken care of."

The interview with Callum Martin had been a marathon. The DCI sat back and consulted with Sergeant Barnes as he prepared himself to face Elizabeth and Edward Greenhalgh.

"What do you think, Harry? Shall we see the mother or the son first?"

"I'd suggest the mother, though I don't fancy either of them. They're not exactly happy bunnies."

"More like raging bulls. Get the constable to show her in."

"Yes, Sir. A copy of Martin's statement is currently being prepared for him to sign."

"Good."

Elizabeth Greenhalgh stormed into the interview room, blaring, "This whole business is outrageous."

"I have to agree with you there, Mrs Greenhalgh. Murder is a horrific crime."

The DCI went through the procedures. She was cautioned and charged in connection with the death of her husband, Carlton Greenhalgh, and with conspiring to kill Mr Robert Stevens. She was warned that anything she said would be recorded and could be used in evidence. DCI Yates indicated a chair, "Please take a seat."

Elizabeth Greenhalgh remained standing, one hand poised defiantly against her hip.

"This may take some time, Mrs Greenhalgh. I'd advise you to sit."

Reluctantly she obeyed. "I've already missed my

appointment and have had to cancel my meeting. I hope you know what you're doing, young man? My family's not without influence."

The DCI ignored her remarks and continued, "Have you arranged for your lawyer to be present?"

"He is on his way and should be with us any minute. This has come as an inconvenience to him, too. He is naturally a very busy man."

"Naturally, we are all very busy people. Is there anything you wish to say before he arrives?"

"I think I've already expressed my feelings. This whole affair is disgraceful."

"But you do understand why you are here?"

"It's certainly not a social call, is it? You have made accusations and I intend to answer them."

"That's what we're hoping. Ah, this will be your lawyer." The constable at the door ushered in a tall bespectacled man. "Good afternoon, Mr Hamilton. Your client has already been charged with being concerned in the murder of her husband and of Mr Robert Stevens."

"This is ridiculous, Geoffrey. Will you please sort it out."

"Just calm down, Elizabeth." Hamilton turned to Yates. "I'm in the dark about these events. May I have a few moments with my client, please?"

Elizabeth Greenhalgh and Geoffrey Hamilton were escorted to another room. They returned some minutes later.

Hamilton was shaking his head. "I'm at a complete loss as to why you think my client could be capable of such crimes," he exclaimed.

"We do have sufficient evidence to bring the charges. Now can we proceed with the questioning? Are you ready to record, Sergeant?"

Harry Barnes nodded and switched on the recording machine. "All set, Sir."

Elizabeth Greenhalgh confirmed her name address, age and the interview began.

Faced with Callum Martin's account of events. Yates watched her lawyer cringe and Elizabeth, herself, became more agitated as the facts were revealed.

"You can't believe the evidence of a senile old man. He lives in a fantasy world. That's obvious by the way he's craving publicity and that stupid programme he was on last night. The man doesn't have any idea of the truth so he concocted a story to suit his own purposes. If you're looking for a murderer then Callum Martin is a good candidate. He's insane enough."

"Aren't you forgetting the evidence of the two officers who apprehended you this morning?"

The DCI explained to her lawyer what had happened at Martin's house.

"I'm telling you it's all nonsense. I'd never heard of this Stevens fellow until it was in the papers. I don't know the man. I've never met him, Geoffrey," Elizabeth Greenhalgh stressed .

She protested her innocence throughout the questioning. Her lawyer asked to accompany her back to the remand cell and was granted ten minutes to talk to her before he returned to the interview room to listen to the whole episode again as Edward Greenhalgh was charged and questioned with the murder of both his father and Rob Stevens.

Edward was a lot calmer than his mother, which surprised the Detective Chief Inspector. As the facts unfolded the latter thought a look of resignation could be detected in Edward's face and manner. It was as if he understood he had no defence to put forward and remained silent. Mr Hamilton, who was representing both Edward and his mother, looked grim.

Edward's reply to most questions put to him was the standard one of the guilty, "No comment."

The young man appeared completely drained. Was he thinking of his heavily pregnant wife outside in the reception room? He had called her to tell her he had been apprehended and was on his way to the police headquarters. She had immediately jumped into her car and driven to Laureston and was at that moment being looked after by a woman police officer.

"Is there anything you would like to add, Mr Greenhalgh?" DCI Yates asked as the interview drew to an end.

He shook his head and was escorted from the room.

DCI Yates had a brief conversation with Mr Hamilton before the latter went to speak to Edward in his remand cell. The lawyer looked every bit as devastated as his clients.

Yates and Sergeant Barnes adjourned to the DCI's office, a spacious well furnished room compared to the space they had shared at Fisborough. Tea and sandwiches were ordered. The investigating officers had missed lunch though the accused had been given refreshments.

"As always it's a sorry mess. So many lives shattered, the victims and the perpetrators. I guess we're the only ones to come out as winners. Martin solved our cases for us. His lawyer has, at his request, handed over the letter he deposited with his office. I arranged for it to be picked up and brought here and Martin's lawyer has arranged to meet with him tomorrow morning.. I can find no flaws in the rest of his evidence. It all appears to work out."

"I've a feeling Edward's about to crack. Funny really, I

thought he'd be the strong one of the pair," Harry Barnes observed.

"The mother's instinct is coming out. She's protesting to protect her son as much as herself. But they're both guilty, all right. It's a cut and dried case. Martin's just as bad. He knew what he was doing when he set up Stevens. He's got history, too. Two charges of assault about fifteen years ago. Martin's no angel."

"His obsession about joining the golf club clouded his thinking and his judgment. His dream's not going to become a reality, now or in the future," Harry said.

"Martin's acted like a fool. I realised that when I suggested the person he'd allegedly seen at the practice area was wearing blue trousers. I was making it up, of course, but he jumped on it and I think in his mind he came to believe it was true. That's what started me thinking about him seriously. He even repeated it on the TV show."

"Edward was dead clever to conceive the notion of a second killing as a diversion."

"Yes, he probable reads a lot of crime books, but it very nearly worked. I wonder, was it his idea or his mother's?"

"It will probably come out at their trial."

"I expect you're right. I wonder what Grant Mason will make of all this? I understand he's leaving for the States in a day or two."

"If he's any sense, he'll reckon he's had a lucky escape. I'm more concerned about young Mrs Greenhalgh and her baby."

DCI Yates shook his head. "It's a sorry business, all right, and there's a lot of distress still to come."

"Shall I get back to Fisborough station, Sir? I guess this is when you and I stop working together."

"Not quite, Harry. We've to tie up the loose ends and I

reckon we owe it to the golf club to go and speak to them personally and, of course, we'll need to notify Stevens' daughter as promised. Hang on for a bit and I'll be ready to leave with you."

At this point Geoffrey Hamilton knocked on the door of the office. "Excuse me, is it convenient for us to talk?"

"I think we can spare a few minutes."

The three men sat at the desk. "I've just left Edward Greenhalgh. He is in quite a state concerning his mother. He was anxious to point out that he, not she, inflicted the fatal blows to both his father and Mr Stevens and is seriously considering making a full written confession in exchange for her release from custody."

"Well now, that's very noble of him, I'm sure, but the law doesn't work that way. Elizabeth Greenhalgh is being charged on a number of counts, including assault, inflicting bodily harm and intimidation. Even a full confession from Edward cannot eradicate those charges. We have to detain her."

"I tried to tell the boy that would be your decision and I understand your ruling. He doesn't seem to regard her involvement as all that serious."

"You'll have to enlighten him on your next visit. Thank you for keeping us informed."

Geoffrey Hamilton left.

"At least Edward Greenhalgh seems prepared to admit his guilt," Harry Barnes observed.

"In view of Martin's statement, he could hardly come up with a denial. No doubt he'll plead mitigating circumstances or something similar. See you in the car park in about twenty minutes, Harry. You can cool your heels in the canteen till then."

"Okay, Raymond. I'll collate some of my notes."

CHAPTER 18

The drive back to Fisborough Police Station was without incident. Yates and Barnes exchanged views on the day's happenings and agreed they were satisfied the case would be concluded. The verdicts of guilty were just a formality in view of the evidence. Detective Superintendant Carter was informed and expressed his satisfaction and congratulated the team.

"Now I can concentrate on mother's plans for my party. Not that I want to celebrate my fortieth, but like Edward Greenhalgh, I feel the need to support my mother. We have that much in common."

"Mary and I are looking forward to the night out and so are the rest of the team, including Pauline Fergus. Did you know she's finished with that rugby player?" Yates nodded and Harry continued, "She's yours for the taking if you ask me. You'd make a handsome couple."

The DCI laughed. "Turning matchmaker are you? Well I want to suggest a different kind of match. Let's get down to Fisborough Golf Club where Clive Meechan will be waiting to be filled in, no doubt. They promised me a game and I fancy booking it. "

At the golf club the news of the arrests was greeted with shock and disbelief, but members expressed relief that the cases were apparently solved. The Ladies' Section was in disarray, and there were mixed feelings about immediately enforcing Elizabeth's resignation as Vice-Captain, with Philippa Hawksworth saying she felt they should wait until the mother and son had been proved guilty before taking any steps. Everyone, including, the staff agreed it would take a long time for the club to recover.

"I'd a feeling Elizabeth and that son of hers had something to do with it from the very start. And as for Callum Martin, he's been a time bomb for months," Sheenagh Davis declared, knowingly.

On the Friday, the day before Yates's big party, a small crowd of golfers gathered to watch the Detective Chief Inspector, Sergeant Barnes and PC Thomas step on to the first tee and prepare to drive off on their long anticipated game. All three sent their balls down the fairway and were about to follow when James Winter came running towards them.

"You've a call from your headquarters. The local station told them where to catch you. It's urgent," He told the DCI.

Reluctantly, Yates took the call in Winter's office while the other officers waited patiently beside the tee. A few minutes later, DCI Yates returned. His demeanour was serious.

"What is it?" Harry asked.

"Edward Greenhalgh has signed a full confession. Unfortunately, he hanged himself in his cell shortly afterwards."

"Oh my God," Harry exclaimed. "His poor wife. I suppose this means we'll have to abandon our game?"

The DCI didn't hesitate as he replied, "I share your concerns, Harry, for young Mrs Greenhalgh and her unborn child. But you know, lads, at this moment there's not a thing we can do to make it better for her. She's receiving counselling and her family will rally round. We've earned this opportunity to relax. So, what's keeping us? Come on."

Raymond Yates led the way down the first fairway. Nothing, he determined, would spoil this game.

#############

Author's note

Thank you for reading Club Force, I hope you enjoyed it. If so, I would be very grateful if you'd leave me a rating and review of the book.

Please go to the book's Amazon pageto do this.

If you have any comments or feedback you'd like to make more directly then please email me at: -

info@authorway.net

Also by Pamela Duncan

On the Swing of One Star

Her mother is killed in the London Blitz. Her father is lost at sea whilst serving in the Merchant Navy. Approaching her 16th birthday, Angie Bolton faces life without the guidance of her parents.

But her father has left her a legacy. A legacy of dreams they shared and it proves to be her driving force as she strives to carve a road for herself against a background of the aftermath of war.

She is disillusioned with life in London with Uncle Cyril, whom she detests, and Edwina Ferrie, his housekeeper, whom she distrusts.

A chance encounter with Lynn Arnold opens a door to luxury and a world to which Angie doesn't feel she belongs. It is a world that offers fun, love and tragedy in equal measure, but could it also hold the key to her fulfilling her aspirations?

ON THE SWING OF ONE STAR is a tale that captures the imagination as it tackles the complexities faced by an adolescent growing up quickly in a changing environment. Inevitably, mistakes are made and lessons learned and many battles of conscience fought but, ultimately, this is a moving account of a young girl's endeavours to let go of her late father by achieving their shared dreams.

The Secret of the Long Room

Take an old Victorian house full of surprising features. Add a lively family of four children, plus parents, of course. Stir in a mischievous friend and a dog called Chips and spice it all up with mysterious, ghostly happenings and you have the ingredients that make up "THE SECRET OF THE LONG ROOM.

14 yr old Hannah Goodsbody guides you through this story of family life with added extras. Written for 9 to 13 year olds this intriguing tale is an irresistible read. Don't miss out.

About the author

A former local reporter, Pamela Duncan has previously published two novels - On The Swing of One Star and The Secret of the Long Room, and two anthologies of poetry - Soul Search and October's Sun. Club Force is her first venture into crime fiction.

About Author Way Limited

Author Way provides a broad range of good quality, previously unpublished works and makes them available to the public on multiple formats.

We have a fast growing number of authors who have completed or are in the process of completing their books and preparing them for publication and these will shortly be available.

Please keep checking our website to hear about the latest developments.

Author Way Limited

www.authorway.net

Made in the USA
Charleston, SC
19 August 2015